DARK

PROMISE

Book Thirteen of the Hayle Coven Novels

PATTI LARSEN

ALSO BY
patti Larsen

The Hayle Coven Universe

The Hunted Series
Fiona Fleming Cozy Mysteries
The Nightshade Cases
The Clone Chronicles
The Diamond City Trilogy
Didi and the Gunslinger

and much, much more.
Find your new favorite author at
pattilarsen.com
Sign up for new releases
bit.ly/pattilarsenemail

CHAPTER ONE

I sucked at packing. Didn't matter how much time I had to tackle the task, my clothes always ended up scrunched and squished and wrinkled. If I stuffed in one more useless sweater the zipper on my long-suffering suitcase would bust. And I still had a week before I had to leave for Harvard.

Restless, I went through my closet again, just in case I forgot something important. The sound of laughter from the living room downstairs drifted up and through my open bedroom door, enticing, but not enough to keep my slightly fractured attention. I could have gone down and sat with Gram and Meira. Sprawled for Sass to sit on my stomach. Privately giggled at how stiff and formal Charlotte held herself even when relaxing in front of a movie, but I just couldn't make myself sit still.

The nightmares and sleeplessness weren't helping. I

felt as though something lived under my skin, crawling around at the least opportune moments, giving me nuclear goosebumps at the mere thought of fangs and blood and cold stars... I shook myself and went deeper, digging through clothes I forgot I had that would probably fit Meira better than me. Funny, this was the first time our coven stayed put for as long as I could remember. No more moving suddenly in the middle of the night, forced to wipe normal's memories and running for the hills because someone in the coven let magic slip. Nope, I was tied to this house and to Wilding Springs for the rest of my life—or as long as the Wild Hunt slept in the backyard. Which, thanks to my immortality, would be about the same length of time.

Sigh. No thinking. Just digging. I giggled over a pair of pale blue leggings with fur on the bottoms and tossed them over my shoulder, followed by a sequined halter-top and a pair of very ugly shoes with bows for toes. But even the unusual finds from my walk-in weren't enough to keep my attention for long. I finally shut the door and sank to the corner of my bed, shoulders slumped, heart beating a little faster than I liked.

—clammy lips on my neck, the sharp jab of fangs, everything going dark—

My entire body jerked as I sat up straight, both hands pressed to my chest as I forced myself to breathe slowly. Batsheva had almost defeated me, would have killed me if not for my slow evolution to becoming maji. Now Sunny was ensconced as the Queen of the Wilhelm clan, Uncle Frank beside her as her Prince, the squabbles of the vampires were over. Or, most of them, I hoped. And it brought me great comfort knowing the shell of Batsheva Moromond sat in my basement, probably gathering mold. Still alive. Suffering.

Fantabulous.

Still.

I stood and paced toward my dresser, hands shoved in my pockets. This inability to relax was getting on my nerves. All I needed was one good night's sleep. Could it be I was so hooked in to trouble when things calmed down I couldn't handle it? I hugged myself, forcing my butt into my desk chair, wiggling my mouse to lose myself in the Internet for a little while.

No thinking.

Social media held zero attraction. Everyone I encountered seemed too damned cheery with their relationship statuses and stupid funny animal pics. My emails had been piling up, though, so I took some time to delete the countless offers for gambling, Viagra, and finding true love in a foreign country while writing back to my friends who took the time to check in on me.

Tippy's lurid tales of her summer fun made me laugh out loud. The young witch I'd met in my first year at college never failed to amuse me. Better. Leave it to the sultry redhead to distract me. I answered her with the suggestion she take up writing romance novels before moving on to one from Quaid.

Syd,

Sorry I couldn't be at the wedding, would have liked to be there. Had a chance to go on an assignment and took it. I hope you understand. See you at school.

Love, Q

Understand? My temper sizzled through my demon's magic and almost fried my keyboard. Yeah, I understood. Sunny and Uncle Frank's recent wedding wasn't nearly as important as some random chance to advance Quaid's budding career. The Enforcers and his life came before family. There was a time when our feelings on such matters were different, when all he craved was family and I wanted out of mine. And while he claimed the Enforcers were his family now, I wasn't buying it.

Nothing mattered as much as the people I loved.

And what was this "love, Q" business? I calmed down, drawing deep breaths, sitting back before my angry fingers could type a very pissed-off reply I'd regret later. I knew he loved me. I loved him, too. But there were times it seemed our priorities were just so out of sync we'd never get it right.

Not that being with him long term was an option anyway. Which led my mind to the maji, my immortality, the vampires.

Twitch. No. Thinking.

I filed his email away for a bit, not ready to answer it in any manner that wouldn't start a fight I wasn't really interested in having. Instead, I clicked on the next in line, eyes flickering over the subject heading while my whole body went tense.

Sydlynn,
You still owe me for saving your life.

Oh. My. Swearword.

Ameline.

Everything inside me screamed denial, from my demon's roar to Shaylee's shriek to my vampire's rumbling anger. Even the family magic bubbled and swirled in answer. No. Way. I didn't owe her anything. I didn't ask her to help me when Batsheva and her clan drained me, stealing the essence of my vampire from me. I was doing just fine on my own.

Yeah. Just fine. Right, Syd. As much as it hurt, ached, burned, part of me knew Ameline was right.

Damn her. Damn her.

My eyes kept reading while my brain spun in furious circles.

Despite the fact I'd rather take the debt directly from you at some point, I've discovered the means to balance the score without your participation. Consider us even.
Best,
Ameline.

Um, what? Cold sweat leaped to the surface of my skin as my heart skipped once, a thudding beat bringing a moment of darkness. The email was time stamped only a half hour ago.

What was she up to? What had she done?

And why the warning?

Panic gripped me even as I felt a surge of demon magic below me.

Dad. Had to be a coincidence, right? Choosing this exact moment to call me when I'd just spoken to him this morning, and everything had seemed fine.

Had to be.

I ran out my door, down the stairs, pounding around the corner and to the basement door, while Meira called, "Syd, is that Dad," her footfalls following me. Sassafras's mind touched mine, but I didn't have time to talk to him, to give him anything.

Ameline couldn't have hurt Dad. He was on Demonicon. This was a fluke.

Just a fluke.

I skidded to a halt after almost falling the last three steps, staring in fear at Dad's diamond effigy. Mom covered it when Dad was forced to break their mating after being tricked into taking Second Seat. But I'd been in steady contact with him since then, refusing to cut him out of my life.

He was still my father.

The demon magic hovered, wavering in the still air of the basement, directly over the pentagram outlined on the concrete floor. But no Dad. I reached for him, panic dimming a little. This was crazy. Ameline was messing with my head. I was right, just a coincidence after all.

"Syd?" Meira stopped on the bottom step, a frown creasing her forehead as amber fire flamed in her eyes. "Was that Dad?"

I didn't answer, turning back from glancing her way, focused on the magic I felt, the surge typically preceded his arrival. But no one called him. If it was Dad, why didn't the power floating in the dimness go to his effigy? I reached for it, let my demon sniff around the touch that brought me downstairs.

The moment I touched the demon magic pooled in the quiet basement, the veil jerked open and powerful amber fire wrapped around me. I heard Meira calling my name, Sassafras, Charlotte's choked cry, only to hurtle headfirst through the tear in the barrier between planes and land on my hands and knees on cold stone. The sizzling crack of the veil sealing behind me was so loud I almost cried out, breathless enough I managed only a whimper.

Thick black nails with red-tinted skin supported me as I pushed myself up, once again in demon form, and looked around, surprise making me dizzy. The large room was dark and chill, outlines of black furnishings familiar, as were the two massive windows I faced.

Ahbi's room. My demon grandmother. It had to have been her power I felt. Anger bubbled as I let my temper burn away the last of my shock. How dare she just pull me across like that? My eyes roved the room, ready to give her hell for such audacity.

My eyes continued scanning as I rose to my feet, feeling my demon surge inside, my vision improving immediately in the darkened room. My anger faded as I ran my hands over goosebumps rising on my arms. The room was silent, empty, the air dead and quiet. I turned slowly, tingling fear traveling up from my toes and making me shudder.

I finished my turn with a gasp as I finally made out a large shape collapsed on the floor, sliver braid spun out behind her.

"Ahbi!" I was moving before I knew it, stumbling to fall on my abused knees at her side, where my grandmother laid facedown. I reached for her, desperate to help her without knowing what was wrong, pulling her toward me, feeling something hot and slick on my skin. I jerked away on impulse, stomach knotted at the scent of copper now very familiar to me.

Looked down.

Choked on a sob of disbelief.

My hands were covered in blood.

chapter two

No. This couldn't be happening. Ahbi was immortal. But even as I stared down at the hot wetness on my trembling hands, I heard her groan, her body trembling ever so slightly, pulling my attention from the life leaking from her to pool on the floor.

"Grandmother!" My life with her flashed through my head, the short and tempestuous relationship we'd shared. How she'd manipulated me, my sister. My father. Forced me to stay on Demonicon and fight for status, all to create a situation where Dad would have no choice but to accept Second Seat. Her powerful will, pure political soul, all of it.

Forgotten. Animosity fled, anger, all that had gone on between us prior to this moment. I reached for her yet again as I rolled her sideways, my world in a slow motion horror film of desperation, until she collapsed on her back, face turning toward me. The light of four moons shone through the window, lighting her eyes, though the life in them faded fast. Her fire died even as I watched, my hands searching her body, struggling to find the source of the giant pool of blood staining the front of her robes.

"Sydlynn." Her hissing whisper ended in a gasp as I fumbled over an impossibly large rent in her chest, through her elegant robe, through her flesh. I flinched from the touch of the wound before clamping my already drenched hands over the gaping hole on the right side of her chest. How was she still alive? Bubbles escaped through my fingers as her laboring lung gushed hot liquid over my skin. The scent of charred meat and fabric rose from the hole in my grandmother, tainted with the heavy tang of magic.

"Hold on, Grandmother, stay with me." I think I was sobbing. It was hard to tell as I fought to keep her blood inside her with my hands and my magic even as my mind reached for Dad. But Ahbi's wards, her safety and privacy, were too strong for me to break through, so old and with so much power invested, they didn't need her to sustain themselves any longer.

Even with her dying in my arms.

"Sydlynn." Softer this time, but more insistent. Magic was getting me nowhere, the taint of whoever hurt her rebuffing all of my efforts to heal the horrible wound. I tried to rise, to run for help, my mind fighting me as panic jerked my attention from my grandmother to the door and her guards. Where were they? Why hadn't they protected her?

"Help!" My voice warbled as I tried to scream while Ahbi's hand grasped mine and her nails dug in, the connection between us tacky with her blood as she pulled my focus back to her.

"Listen." Flames flickered in her amber eyes, face collapsing as she faded from me. But her heart, her soul, refused to quit until her message was delivered. "Thought it was you. Witch magic."

Oh. My. Swear—

Ameline.

This is what she meant. Ameline tricked my grandmother into thinking she was me. And then attacked her.

The. Bitch. Would. Die.

"Find her." My hand burned under Ahbi's grip, an amber tinted glow flaring between us as her hand tightened, the twitch of dying reflex and absolute refusal to fail. "Avenge me." I cried out in agony as what felt like a lance of pure fire raced up my arm and jabbed me in the heart. Gasping for air, I collapsed over Ahbi's body, tears blinding me a moment as much as the pain. I blinked them away, chest heaving as the hurt eased, my lips brushing her cheek as she smiled, a tiny smile. "So proud," she mouthed.

And was gone.

A heartbeat of silence followed before I hitched in a breath of disbelief.

And then, a giant column of magic burst from her chest, rising into the darkness of the room, lighting it with the glare of a harsh Demoniconian sun before the power spun into a tornado of blazing fire and shot through the door, shattering the heavy wood in every direction. I ducked some shrapnel, hunched over Ahbi to keep her safe, though she no longer needed such protection.

Would never need it again.

Her personal wards hummed their own discord of agony and began to shatter, bursting into tiny flames around me as the power she'd given them followed her death. Fireworks of exploding shielding cascaded over me, sending me to once again fall over my grandmother in a vain attempt to protect her fallen body.

I gasped for air, unable to move as the last of the wards died with her, rocking Ahbi's body gently, frozen by shock and, to my surprise, real grief over her loss. She was a hard-assed politician, but she was also my grandmother.

I almost missed the ghostly shape as it lifted from her cooling flesh, rising in a fog of amber magic, winding into its own mini twister of burning energy before slamming into me, rocking me back away from her empty shell.

Demon magic raced through my veins, flooding me with power, her personal power. Ahbi's magic left to me, in the end.

It was a struggle to sit up as my demon roared and swelled inside me, gathering the new magic to herself, fighting for possession of my body. Her rage battered my mind, her need to find Ameline and tear her apart so powerful she drove me to my hands and knees, trying to force me to stand before Shaylee and my vampire corralled my demon and allowed me room to breathe.

Not much room as I bent over Ahbi and kissed her forehead, resting my cheek there a moment while I gathered my thoughts.

I should have known the thundering magic of Demonicon rushing to find its new host would finally draw attention, but my mind simply wouldn't pull together in any coherence. Not until Pagomaris and a flood of Guards thundered through the shattered entry into Ahbi's suite, skidding to a halt and staring at me with open horror, all of them.

"Ruler!" My grandmother's faithful aide wailed the title as Pagomaris rushed forward and collapsed beside Ahbi. She sobbed herself when she finally accepted the loss, knowing in one look at Ahbi's damaged and empty body, her Ruler was gone.

"Pagomaris," I whispered, reaching for her, only to have the normally kind and efficient demon pull away from me with fury written all over her face.

"Sydlynhamitra," she half-snarled, half-sobbed. "What have you done?"

chapter three

I paced in my tiny cell, buried at the bottom of the Seat, deep under the mountain while my mind whirled and argued and fought for focus.

Pagomaris hadn't given me even a second to explain. "How could you?" She gasped as I reached for her with Grandmother's magic, wanting her to understand I had nothing to do with her beloved Ruler's death.

But Pagomaris took the touch the wrong way.

"How despicable," she hissed, hovering over the body as though I tried to take Ahbi's physical form away from her adoring aide. "Murdering your own blood and stealing her power for your own. You disgust me. Guards!" I trembled as I tried to put two words together, heart screaming "No!" while my lips opened and closed in silence even as a pair of giant demons in uniforms grabbed me and clamped stone shackles around my hands.

The moment the restraints closed over my skin my whole magical world went dark. Every bit of it. No power. Where was my power? I fought them at last, screaming wordlessly, body twisting as they carried me away, still shrieking, mind contracting as I tried to make them understand while the loss of my magic drove me to the brink.

Demons stared, some with rage, others with despair, a few with nasty smiles on their faces as I was tossed onto the elevator, sliding dangerously close to the edge. One of my feet impacted the humming shield surrounding the lift even as my mind, now overloaded with terror at the thought of falling added to everything else, completely shut down.

I woke in my cell, head pounding, mouth parched, a burning need aching in my gut and heart even as I rolled off the edge of a narrow metal plate, falling with a grunt of pain on my hands and knees for the second time on the icy stone floor.

My stomach heaved, bile exiting in a rush, though whatever I'd had for dinner was either long gone or hadn't traveled with me. And while I let my brain wander off, wondering if what I ate did cross the veil or if my demon body was totally separate, I huddled against the wall with my still-shackled hands over my knees and cried myself hoarse.

How had this happened? How had I gone from packing for school to being locked up, power blocked, accused of murdering my own grandmother? I tried to reach for Dad, rational thoughts brief and fleeting. At least part of me remained aware through the growing sense of urgency inside me and the terrible, aching emptiness of where my power used to be. Almost too aware of the horrible truth facing me.

I wasn't guilty, no way, no how. Power or no power, proving my innocence, offering evidence, had to come first. I gritted my teeth and jerked myself under some modicum of control.

No luck with Dad. No power, remember? Okay then. Gotcha. Take stock. I was alive. Wicked. Count that as a win for the home team. A little worse for wear, but intact. I scrubbed at the crusted, dark mess still coating my hands, flakes of Grandmother's blood falling from my skin to the damp floor while I shuddered continually. Stop that. Big girl panties, put them on. My head impacted the wall behind me as I closed my eyes and forced myself to breathe. Dad would never believe I killed her. So stop being an idiot. And any second now, he'd be down here, breathing fire, to rescue me. So chin up, kiddo.

I'd handled worse.

Oh, but I hadn't, had I? At least back home I had those I could rely on to save me if I needed help. Here, on Demonicon, accused of killing their beloved leader, with only my father on my side—if he even was, what the hell kept him?—and every other demon out there ready to strip me of power at the first opportunity, my very limited window of salvation seemed narrow indeed.

Theridialis. Sassy's dad. Right, yeah. Buddy number two. He'd never believe it either.

I couldn't sit there anymore, shaking so hard my teeth rattled together, clearly in shock. I had to get up, start moving, if only to warm my freezing body, toes and fingertips losing feeling from the cold. Hands tucked under my arms, wishing I'd been wearing a winter coat instead of my t-shirt and pajama bottoms when I'd run headfirst into disaster. I paced in my bare feet, swearing when I got home—no way I'd even consider "if" as my mind seized on the word and wailed—I would wear the fuzzy socks Gram gave me for Christmas every day and be grateful for them.

It felt like forever since I'd woken, an age, a lifetime. Were they planning to leave me down here to starve, rot away in my own filth? I clutched at my stomach and chest as the intensity of my pain increased. Odd, it seemed to fade as I drew closer to the door and grow stronger when I turned back. Finally, something to latch onto, a little mystery to explore and keep me sane.

Yes, not my imagination or anything. I pressed my hands to the cold metal door, even reaching up on my tiptoes to wiggle my fingers out the narrow bars at the top, the only opening. Though the pressure didn't vanish, it eased enough I noticed it. But the moment I backed away, I doubled over as a spike of red-hot fire jammed me in the guts and my heart constricted.

I sank to the metal slab, tears trickling down my cheeks as the pain slowly eased, but didn't fade completely. That's where I was crouched when someone shouted on the other side of the door just before it clanged open to slam into the rock wall, ringing like a giant bell of doom.

"Sydlynn!" Dad rushed to me, gathered me into his arms. I collapsed against him, sobbing again, clutching the front of his robe as best I could with my hands shackled together, the open doorway calling me toward a golden light and freedom.

Home.

"Dad." I gasped for air, caught my breath, slapped myself mentally. "Dad, I didn't kill Grandmother. You have to believe me."

"Of course I believe you," he whispered. Spun with a snarl of rage. "Why is her power blocked?"

One of the Guards wavered before shrugging. "Orders, my lord."

Dad froze, face turning to stone. The Guard's face suddenly flushed as he fell to his knees.

"Forgive me, Ruler," he choked as his body lifted

from the ground, grasped in a fist of amber magic before crashing to the floor with a horrible crunching sound.

"That's the last time you'll make that mistake," Dad growled as I clung to him, all the while wondering what he'd become. A crack of magic, so loud I let out a meep of fear, shattered the stone holding my hands together—

—here, we're here, are you all right? We're here with you now.

My powers, vampire, Sidhe, demon, calling for me, catching in mid-cry, embracing me even as Dad embraced me, flooding me with their magic while I hugged myself inside the circle of my father's arms and rocked in relief, more tears leaking down my cheeks.

Damned tears.

"Syd." Dad let me go, took my hands in his, flinching at the flecks of blood I'd failed to remove. "You need to let me in so I can see what happened."

Yes, yes of course. I threw my defenses wide, opening to him completely. I was sure in my need for him to find what he was looking for I showed him a few things I'd be embarrassed my dad knew about later. But, for the moment, there could be nothing between us.

I was there again, in the basement at home, Dad beside me as he followed me through memory.

She called you? Dad felt the magic as I reached for the pool of it hovering over the pentagram. Was pulled through it again. He fell with me on the polished floor, looked around when I did. Crawled to Ahbi. Looked at my bloody hands. Heard her last whispered words, saw the transfer of magic as she told me to avenge her and watched, face cold and dark, as the magic of Demonicon rose in a rush and thundered away.

To you? Had to be. He felt so powerful now, more powerful than ever. Like his mother had been.

To me. He waited, finally showing some emotion when Ahbi's personal power left her and entered me, my struggle to rise and follow the pressure I now felt inside.

Syd, Dad sent. *Oh, Syd. How could she?*

A tear tracked down his cheek as together in the memory we bent to kiss Ahbi's forehead just before Pagomaris stormed in.

Ameline did this, Dad, I sent as we surfaced. "She even told me she planned it." I stammered my way through telling him about the email, words choked around a throat so tight I thought I'd lose my ability to speak any moment. "This is all my fault."

"But how did she cross?" Dad shook his head. "If it was Ameline, she needed a demon form to enter, Syd."

"She found a way." I was certain of it. There was no other explanation, not after what Ahbi told me about witch magic. "She's obsessed with becoming maji."

"I have to leave you." Dad stood, face hardening, but sadness in his eyes. "I'm sorry, sweetheart. Until you've been cleared by a tribunal, I can't release you. As much as I know you're innocent."

21

What the...? No. Freaking. Way.

"Dad!" I stood, went after him as my energy wrapped around me, Ahbi's magic driving me toward the door. "What did you mean, how could she? What did Grandmother do to me?"

"Just stay put," he said. "I'll convene the tribunal immediately. You'll be out of here and on your way home in no time. Trust me, cupcake." His fingers stroked my cheek. "I'm sorry, but there's so much more to this than you know. I have no options."

The door clanged shut behind him with such finality I simply stood there, trembling, waiting for him to come back. He had to come back. He couldn't just abandon me like this.

Could he?

My pacing recommenced while a new argument started up.

Let's just leave. Shaylee had found her voice. She chose to speak so rarely I almost jumped when she piped up. *This is a terrible circumstance. We have enough collective power to open the veil and go home.*

She was right, we did. My demon roared her protest.

We have to stay. She hadn't spoken to me since we'd come together again the night we put the Wild Hunt to bed, and I found I'd missed her voice. Only now it was tinged with another's. With Ahbi's. *We have an oath to fulfill.*

I didn't swear any oath, I snapped at her. Ahbi asked, but

I didn't say anything. Did I? My panicked mind went back through the conversation, stumbling over Ahbi's dying words. But I was sure I was right.

It appears that doesn't matter, my vampire said in her calm and gentle voice. *From what I understand of the pressure you're now under—with you thanks to our association—the geas Ahbi Sanghamitra placed on you was done without you needing to consent.*

So that's what Dad meant. Leave it to Ahbi to saddle me with some revenge oath. She should have trusted me to kill Ameline anyway. That was my plan, after all.

No need for demonic death pacts.

We have to leave. My demon paced in my head. *The evil one will escape us. She can't escape us.*

Got that one, loud and clear, I sent. *Let me guess, since I'm not entirely new to this rodeo: if we don't fulfill this oath?*

We will die, my demon sent.

Craptastic.

CHAPTER FOUR

Again, it seemed like forever went by while I discarded urge after urge to break out of my cell and go hunting. I only succeeded in keeping my demon in check thanks to the combined power of my vampire, Shaylee and my witch magic, even as the urgency of the imposed oath slowly built in pressure until I felt certain my chest would explode.

More voices behind the door spun me around, eagerly reaching for Dad, lurching to the exit. Only to find myself clutching, not at my father, but the sadly smiling Theridialis.

"Sydlynn, dear girl," he said as he hugged me to his portly body while the door closed on us. "How are you holding up?"

How was I holding—?!? He was lucky I had a firm

grasp on my demon or he'd be prone on the floor and likely unconscious for a very long time.

"I take it that means you're not here to let me out." Clenched teeth served me well yet again. At this rate, I'd be wearing dentures by the age of twenty-five from all the grinding I'd done over the years.

"I'm afraid not." He released me, sagging, round belly a wave of jiggles as his head fell forward, mouth pulling down at the corners. "Things are not going well, Sydlynn. I came to warn you."

Um, what? "Dad has proof I didn't kill Grandmother," I said.

"While that is true," he said, "there is other proof being presented before the tribunal, a great deal of it, in fact. And since your father's word can't be unbiased..."

"He's Ruler," I snapped. "His word should be good enough."

"I agree." Theridialis sighed, sitting gingerly on the edge of my metal bunk, the bolts holding it to the wall groaning under his weight. "But there are many who oppose your father, Sydlynn. Who see him as weak, no true replacement for his mother. And who now circle like *kaftaka* with fresh blood in the water."

I didn't know what a *kaftaka* was, but sharks and razor teeth seemed to fit the bill.

Theridialis burst into tears, chubby hands covering his face. I tried to sit beside him, but didn't want to risk the bunk collapsing beneath us. Instead, I patted his back, feeling very weird I was comforting him when it was my ass on the line.

"My own ex-mate," he choked at last, "speaks against you." He looked up, amber eyes bloodshot and glowing in his grief. "I know not why she lies, or what her agenda is, but my heart is broken, Sydlynn. Sassafras's mother and I have known each other for centuries. This is a betrayal of all we've ever stood for."

Considering in what low esteem Sass held his mom, I found Theridialis's reaction odd, but continued to pat his back. "Does she have a lot of sway?" This could be very bad.

"She does," he said. "Though never with Ahbi herself. With other demons who have craved Ruler's power for a very long time."

"Her word against mine." I shook my head, trying to calm my pounding heart. "I'll win, Theridialis."

"That's just the thing," he whispered. "She showed us the murder, Sydlynn. And it was your magic that killed Ahbi."

Excuse me, please? "Hell, no."

"Hell, yes." He snuffled, wiping his face on the sleeve of his elaborate robe. "Let me show you." One hand clamped over my wrist as Theridialis's mind opened and I found myself thrust into the same familiar scene.

But this one was different. My grandmother stood at

her desk, reading something she'd etched in fire before her. I felt a surge of magic—witch magic, definitely— watched as Ahbi stood with a smile, gesturing as she cleared her working space and approached the window, the veil tearing open.

I stepped through the gap, power flaring in my hands as I crossed, impacting Grandmother's chest. She cried out, reached for me as she fell. I approached her, kicked her with one foot until she rolled on her side, and then her face, groaning.

Grinning, I spun and left the scene.

"Wait!" I jerked my hand free of Theridialis's grip, lungs collapsing as I fought for air, more sobs trying to surface while I struggled with what I'd just witnessed. "That wasn't me."

"I know it wasn't," he said. "But it looked like you, and the witch magic made it feel like you. To the tribunal, that could be enough."

"This is a trick." Fiery anger finally surged and I let it, feeling it engulf me as I spun away from the unhappy demon, my own howling her fury. Almost time to let her out. "Ameline set me up."

"Your father mentioned this witch you've fought in the past," Theridialis said. "And that you think she is the cause of Ahbi's death?"

I turned back, hardly hearing him while I tried to formulate a plan of escape. I couldn't stay here any longer. I'd done this song and dance one too many times and wasn't sure even my particular invincibility would protect me if it came to a guilty verdict. Humans might burn witches and vampires drain their own dry, but demons had particularly dark hearts and I had no desire to be stripped of my magic, turned into a drooling, empty shell and disposed of in the heart of the mountain's magma core.

Nope. Nope. No thanks.

Theridialis still waited for an answer to his question. "Ameline did this," I said. I know she did." My eyes met Theridialis's amber gaze. "I need to talk to Dad." This was nuts. No more sitting around. Ameline might have pushed me into a corner, but no way was I letting things go any further.

The grief and shock holding me hostage shattered as I let my demon out.

But Theridialis surged to his feet, shaking his head, horror on his face. "No, no, you mustn't." He glanced at the door, as though knowing what I was thinking, hands grasping for me while he turned back to face me. "Please, you mustn't."

"I won't let them strip my power and kill me for something I didn't do," I snarled.

"Nor will I," he whispered. "Or your father. But if you flee now, before you can be heard..." he shook his head, jowls trembling, eyes pleading with me, magic too.

"You must think of your father."

To hell with politics. Dad was a big boy and I wasn't going down for this, no way, no how. But the fear on Theridialis's face made me sigh, stuff my demon back down while she cursed me and kicked at the other magicks holding her in.

Just a few minutes more, I sent her, barely enough of a consolation to calm her, as I clenched my fists around a double handful of Theridialis's robe, reaching for Dad myself only to meet a solid wall of nothing.

"Shields." More teeth clenching. My jaw was getting a wonderful workout. Fine. Whatever. "Tell Dad," I said, since I couldn't do so myself, "he has an hour."

The portly scientist nodded quickly. "I'll tell him," he said. "Once I've cleared the prison level."

And the shields. Lovely.

Theridialis left me to fume. Now that I'd broken free of the dark melancholy and horrible weakness, the oath Ahbi instilled flared to further life, driving me to pace in stomping steps. My feet ached from the impact on the floor, hands clenched so tight I couldn't feel my fingers from lack of circulation. I knew the geas had to be reaching its pressure limit from the tingling racing through me, demanding I pay attention, go after Ameline at once. I had to act soon or, according to my demon, die.

Dying was not on my agenda for tonight.

When the door opened the third time and three

Guards marched in, crowding my little space, I released a relieved gust of air and almost smiled, not in happiness, but because things were finally moving ahead.

"About time," I said.

"It certainly is," one of them answered. And closed the door behind him.

chapᴛᴇʀ ꜰɪᴠᴇ

I should have been expecting an attack. After what Theridialis told me about the hostile environment above, not to mention my previous experience on Demonicon, an attempt on my life was an obvious thing, wasn't it? But, like a doofus, I wasted a precious moment on "huh?" while the three Guards, the closed cell door now shutting out the rest of the world, gathered their power and pounced.

Not for the first time and certainly not for the last, I was grateful for the presence and vigilance of the other powers living with me. Without them, I know my life, as invincible as I might have been, would have likely ended that night.

As it was, my vampire threw out a shining silver shield only just in time to block the first blast of golden fire even as Shaylee's earth magic dove deep under the rock and burst forth, turning the ground beneath the hulking Guards to rubble, driving them to their knees. My demon reacted next, a massive lash of magic whipping through the trio as they howled in pain.

The door clanged open again, impacting one of the Guards in the head, the sound not quite as dramatic as when it struck stone, but infinitely more satisfying as his eyes rolled to white and he collapsed to the ruined floor. The other two Guards, still writhing in agony from the lash my demon delivered, toppled in turn as a pair of masked demons hurtled their own balls of fire. My vampire shield, now reinforced with demon, witch and Sidhe magic, was more than enough to protect me from the flashover, but I winced anyway, brightness of the flames flaring to painful.

I eyed the pair of demons through the sparkling stars dancing in my vision. They stood in my doorway, black masks disguising their features while the three Guards lay suddenly silent at my feet. I wasn't sure if I should be grateful, considering if my two masked visitors were there to rescue me I'd already had the whole thing well in hand.

"Nice timing," I said, not even trying to keep the sarcasm from my voice as I nudged a fallen Guard with one toe. "Now who sent you?"

Neither spoke, just exchanged a look before the first, tall and broad-shouldered, raised his hand to me. Wait a second. His hand wasn't empty. What was he pointing—

A tiny silver projectile sliced through my shields, flaring with magic as it did. Before I could try to muster some kind of defense, the prick of its sting made me wince and brush at it with numb fingers.

Very numb. Hands, too. Arms like lead. I lifted my head, certain it weighed a hundred tons and took a staggering step forward, pulling in my magic as everything slid sideways into darkness.

"—supposed to take her with us." A male voice punctured the black, echoing in my head as I blinked a few times.

Sydlynn, my vampire whispered. *Be silent.*

Silent? Okie dokie. I could do silent. If only the pounding in my head knew what silent meant. Tiny jackhammers of pain worked their way across my skull and settled behind my eyes.

Not a sound, she sent, soothing my pain with spirit power. *Listen.*

I ran my tongue around my parched mouth. *You got it.* The need to giggle was so powerful I bit my lower lip to stop myself. The pain of my teeth clamped on my swollen mouth nearly drew a gasp from me, but it was enough to shatter the edge of the funny fog and bring me the rest of the way into consciousness.

"I don't care what he said," a second voice spoke,

slightly higher pitched, though also male, and a little whiny in my opinion. And I knew whiny. Been there, done that, irritated the hell out of myself in the process.

Sydlynn. The vampire sighed. *I know it's hard, but you have to focus.*

Focus. Where was I? A moment of panic told me all of my powers were with me, though Shaylee and my demon remained out of it.

Let them sleep, my vampire sent. *Especially our demon. She will react badly, and we need to pay attention before she wakes and does something unfortunate.*

Yeah. That was a tactful word. *I'm here,* I sent back, sluggish, lethargic and still on the verge of giggles. *Where are we?*

In some kind of transport, she sent. *We're fleeing Ostrogotho, from what I've gleaned.*

Leaving the Seat? But the tribunal. Dad! Only my vampire's calm collective held me still.

We've been kidnapped, she sent. *But you notice the pain and pressure from Ahbi's geas has gone?*

She was right, it had. *So we're heading in the right direction.*

Perhaps, she sent. *We're moving at least. It may be all the oath requires to still its needs.*

For now. I opened one eye a crack, light pulling my gaze from the dull gray of what had to be a seat to the rim of a shield bubble. Definitely a transport. I'd had some experience with them before, been on a small one with my grandmother when she gave Meira and I a tour of the Planes the last time we were here. *Who are our two friends? Or were there more than two?*

I reached out ever so carefully with my spirit power, tied to my vampire for stability, as I continued to waffle between the need to laugh at nothing in total hysteria and squeezing my aching head in agony.

Only two, she sent. *And young. Some kind of resistance fighters? They've been whispering and I've only just been able to overhear them.*

Fair enough. *There was a resistance building against Ahbi's rule,* I sent as the ghostly thread of spirit whispered over the first demon, giving me the barest visual, like the flashed afterimage of an underdeveloped photograph. But it was enough to fill in the blanks we needed to make a plan.

I lay on a bench, formed from the material of the transport through magic, my back turned to the front of the vehicle. Another long bench separated me from my kidnappers. This transport was obviously designed for larger numbers of demons or even cargo. My abductors sat at the front, the one on the left managing some kind of control board while the demon on the right sat half-turned toward him.

"—disappointed in your lack of conviction." Hang on. I knew that first voice, even kept low and soft. Where had I heard it before?

"He isn't here with us, is he?" The second demon grew more sniveling by the second, voice louder, and I could only imagine he turned his head to look at me. "Smuggling the most wanted demon on any plane out of Ostrogotho?"

"You joined us for a reason," the first voice snapped while I gnawed at my recognition in irritation. I was too young to have such a terrible memory. All those blows to the head and druggings were catching up with me, for sure.

"I'm not a traitor to the cause," number two snapped back. "But no one said anything about this level of risk."

The first laughed, a deep sound vibrating through my muscles and bones as the transport banked softly. "You do realize just being a member of the resistance makes you a traitor to the Seat? That you can be stripped and killed for your choice?"

The other didn't say anything, silent as his partner in crime went on.

"This isn't some tame farmer's *perinathon* ride, Ahmose. Some cause you can dabble in."

"How dare you." The second demon's anger rippled over me as his magic escaped his control.

"Don't be a fool," the first said. "You're no match for me. And we have a job to do. You want to challenge me, Ahmoselurem, you wait until we're on the ground and safe with Leader. Then I'll be happy to tear your pathetic heart out."

Silence reined a moment. *This could go badly*, my vampire sent. *If they can't keep their tempers in check.*

You think? Just what I needed, kidnappers who hated each other's guts.

"She's a liability." The pitch and level of whine increased in demon number two. "You know it. Let's just kill her and dump the body. Her death will serve as well as her captivity."

"No," the first said. "She's our best hope. Now shut up and let me focus. We're coming to the border and I won't have you screwing this up."

The border of the city? Had to be.

If we're going to act, I sent, *we should do it before we cross out of Ostrogotho.*

Agreed, my vampire sent. *But quietly.*

Quietly. I could do quietly.

Would have managed it, certainly. If my demon hadn't chosen that exact moment to wake up.

Snorting, shaking her inner head, without a trace of the giddiness plaguing me. Nope, she was on the far side of the spectrum from laughter. About as far as she could get. As in Miss Cranky-Pants. Pissed off. Ready to tear someone—anyone—to shreds. My vampire and I both fought her, tried to calm her down as she took in the situation and the fact we'd been drugged. But the surge of rage she flooded my body with burned in an

37

uncontrollable fire. Amber lit my vision as my body spun on the bench, my demon bringing us into a crouch, a ball of flaming magic balanced in either hand.

Both demons turned with shock in their faces. "I thought you said she was out for hours!" I paired number two's voice with the image of him, wide through the chest, but weak in the chin, just as my demon roared her unhappiness from my gaping mouth and threw her weapons forward.

The driver dodged to the left, shields absorbing the explosion of magic, but his partner didn't deal with the attack quite so well. His hastily raised protections didn't draw in the power impacting them, but instead sent them on a ricochet, the burning mass of magic blowing a massive hole in the front of the transport as demon number one leaped backward with a cry of fear.

The transport shuddered, nose falling away, taking the control panel with it.

"Are you insane?" The first demon spun on me, his face now connecting to the voice I'd heard, the handsome merchant boy I'd met on my first visit, expression nowhere near the one of wicked attraction I remembered now twisted into anger and terror.

"You kidnapped me," I snarled, my demon speaking through my mouth, but with my permission.

"And you've killed us," he snapped back. "Without the magic controls to stabilize this vessel, we'll crash."

chapter six

The transport, magical support gone, fell like a very bulky and badly shaped stone, the bubble overhead flickering as the last of the power running through the vehicle finally ran out. Freezing wind tackled me as the shield collapsed, sending me backward into what had been a bench seat, now just an empty space, to impact the low lip of the edge of the transport. I was very lucky the side wasn't flat, and that I'd been crouching at the time. Had I been standing, there was no way I would have managed to stay on board. The knee-high ridge barely caught me as it was. Stiff material I could only compare to plastic bruising my ribs, all the air rushing out of me as the non-existent nose of the craft turned down toward the ground.

The two demons slid at me, the boy from the market diving headfirst, hands outstretched to save his head from impacting the edge of the vehicle while his companion grabbed for the only thing he could reach on the way by.

Me.

Hands off, jerktard. Get yourself killed on your own time.

He grasped at my legs as he half-fell over the edge, pulling me sideways. I grunted with the effort it took to hold my place, driving wedges of power through the hull of the ship, anchoring myself with earth and air magic. The clinging demon refused to let go, pulling against my leg, using me as a rope, until he slid in next to me, panting, still clinging to my thigh. His struggle knocked the transport into a slow spin, my stomach protesting as the air changed from bitterly cold to something more temperate.

Oh, goody. I wouldn't be an icicle when I died.

Humor only delayed my panic and the surfacing memory of the last time I'd plummeted to my near death. The endless nightmares about my fall from the elevator, the terror trying to take over even as I fought my mind for control.

—*falling, falling, the city below rushing toward me as my mind screamed in terror*—

The veil, my vampire said, so calm it broke me loose from my memory. I almost laughed, fear turned to insane humor, while the world came closer and closer.

Right. The veil. I snatched at it, my demon eagerly

slicing through. Only to be blocked.

No good, I sent back with as much calm as I could muster. The tapestry of the ground below changing from a distant vista to a detailed, 3D panorama I wouldn't be enjoying much longer.

—falling, falling, screaming, dying—

Sydlynn, she sent. *I know you're scared. But you must act.*

Yup, yup. Had to act. Okay then. A triple jab from vampire, Sidhe and demon, jerked me out of my stunned terror state.

Okay, this was worse. Much worse, but at least panic was familiar enough. Mouth gaping open, screaming out loud now because I couldn't help myself, the pair of demon kidnappers clinging to me as we plummeted to the ground, I called up every ounce of air magic I could muster. My power cocooned us in a bubble, the tip sealing over the shattered nose of the transport the split second before we hit the ground.

I was suddenly weightless, flying up toward the shield, bouncing back from it to hit the bed of the ship so hard I lost my ability to breathe for the second time. Someone's foot hit my knee while my hip crushed a foreign hand, but there was nothing to be done, not while we bounced one more time before sliding, red dust flying around us, blocking the view of outside, for what seemed like forever.

I ground my teeth together, prepared for the worst,

body stiff, waiting for a final impact. When it came, the hissing sizzle of ground passing under our shield fading to a soft hum, the hull barely bumped whatever brought us to a halt at last.

Each breath panted from my aching lungs, my heart pounding so fast it thrummed from the strain at any moment I let the air magic collapse. And instantly regretted it. A cloud of dust and debris rained down on us, drawing cries of protest from my kidnappers while I coughed and waved at the filthy air.

I know I should have leaped to my feet and challenged the pair of them immediately, calling for Dad or some other reinforcement to take the two traitors away. But I couldn't bring myself to move, lying there with a leg draped over mine and someone's chest under my head.

I had a very hard head. I hoped the impact hurt.

Market Boy was the first to stir, half-sitting before falling back again. It was his leg pinning me down and as he rolled on his side and met my gaze, amber eyes glowing with amusement, I wanted to rip that leg off and feed it to him.

"Nice landing," he said. "Fly much?"

He was so lucky I didn't punch him in the nose. "Get off me," I snarled, my demon shoving him aside with her power even as he backed off, hands up, coughing himself as the dust settled. I pushed myself up, not caring the kidnapper trapped under me cried out in pain.

Let him. Served him right.

"I can't believe we're alive." The one named Ahmoselurem stared up at me as I turned to look down, his weak chin wobbling as tears filled his eyes. "You saved us."

"You forget, my friend," Market Boy said with a wink, "she's the one who almost got us killed in the first place."

And I thought Quaid was a jerkasaurus.

"That's it." I scrambled to my feet, hands on hips, ignoring the twinge in my knee from the blow I'd taken, glaring at the pair of them. "You two are in deep doo-doo and there's no way I'm saving your asses again. Not after you had the nerve to kidnap me."

Market Boy shrugged. "So turn us in, Princess," he said.

Argh. Men. Boys, more like it. Screw this. I was going home.

I reached for the veil without thinking and met the same wall, the same resistance. I blurted out a few words I normally didn't use to punctuate my unhappiness while Market Boy continued to smirk at me and his friend wiped filthy tear tracks from his face.

We can't leave, no matter if you were able to open the veil, my vampire said. *Ahbi's power would stop you.*

Damn it. DAMN IT.

Amber light flickered over my sight as I glared at the pair before looking around, expecting to see the towering heights of Ostrogotho.

Nope. No city. What the…?

"I thought we were just clearing the border?" I kicked Market Boy's foot in frustration. "Where the hell are we?"

"The border, yes," he said, climbing to his feet, not offering a hand to his companion who glared at him as he struggled to rise. "The city lies far from the edge of its own territory."

Oh, just freaking lovely. "How far?" I couldn't ride the veil and I wasn't looking forward to walking.

"Far." He dusted himself off. "Too far to walk, if that was what you had in mind."

"Okay," I said, feeling more than a little huffy about the whole disaster and ready to let my demon out just to work off some steam. "So what are you going to do about it?"

"Nothing." Market Boy grinned like it was some kind of giant joke with a punch line I hadn't heard yet. "Not until we talk."

"Oh, you want to talk now." So much sarcasm. I really had to find a way to better vent my anger. Then again, it served me well in the past and just felt so *good*.

"Allow me to introduce myself." He bowed at the waist, an elaborate gesture involving hand movements I barely followed before he straightened again. "I am

Rameranselot. And in case you've forgotten, we've met before."

"I remember," I said. "But you weren't kidnapping me then so I had a little better opinion of you."

"Fair enough." He grinned before gesturing to the other demon who now stood next to him with a scowl on his face. "And this is Ahmoselurem, my steadfast companion in crime."

"Stuff it, won't you, Ram?" Ahmoselurem shrugged off the hand Rameranselot set on his shoulder. "We're nothing of the sort."

"One can dream, my fine friend." Ram's wink almost cracked my sullen shell.

Almost.

"How lovely for you both," I snapped. "Now, do you mind telling me what this is all about?"

"Saving your life," Ram said. "For the second time."

I snorted and shook my head. "Dad would never let them execute me for something I didn't do," I said.

"Sydlynhamitra," Ram said, serious at last, "those three Guards weren't there to give you a dancing lesson. If they failed, another attempt would have been made. And another. Until they succeeded in killing you."

That sounded distinctly demonish, so I bought it, though I wanted very badly to know who was behind the attacks. "On whose orders?"

"We don't know for certain," he said. Naturally. "But

our network knew you were in danger."

Grumble, mumble. "You could have just told me."

"And you would have then walked out with us, climbed into a transport with two total strangers and left Ostrogotho on our word?" Ram's sarcasm equaled mine. Well, not quite. I was better at it. "How silly of me, Princess. I'll remember how easy you are to convince for next time."

"We can't just stand around here talking," Ahmose cut him off, eyes scanning the empty horizon. "The Guards will come after her."

"Good," I said, hopping over the edge of the transport, bare feet squishing into hot sand. It was warming up, the suns now fully risen, and I found myself fanning my face absently with one hand as I looked around.

"Did you hear a word I said?" Ram's anger finally showed up. "We have no way of knowing if the Guards who do come are planning to kill you."

"Planning to *try* to kill me," I said. "Big difference." I had more firepower available to me than ever before, thanks to Ahbi. "I have to go back and talk to Dad. Not to mention the fact, this little breakout idea of yours has probably made me look guilty as hell." I spun on Ahmose. "And don't for a second think I wasn't listening when you said you wanted to kill me." I jabbed an index finger at him as he flinched and stepped behind Ram.

"Watch it."

Ram spun on one heel and shaded his eyes before a small smile broke over his face. "I know where we landed," he said. "There's a settlement not far from here." He turned back, smirking. "As long as Her Highness doesn't mind a little walking, we can reach shelter and hopefully another transport."

"Won't they come looking for us?" Our crash had been rather spectacular, if I did say so myself.

"Not likely," Ram said. "We were disguised until you blew out our systems. No one would think what fell was a transport."

"If they were even watching," Ahmose said, face pulled down into a glum frown.

"I could just reach for Dad right now." Why hadn't I? Because I knew, deep down, Ram was right. Dad would want to send Guards for me. And even if they were loyal to my father, there was still this damned geas of Ahbi's to deal with. Remembering the pain from the cell, how the power drove me to leave, I knew if I tried to turn around, I'd be in big trouble.

But I couldn't just wander off with the two demons who kidnapped me. Could I?

Ram kicked the hull of the transport, mostly buried in sand, before turning and walking off, leaving me behind. Ahmose scowled, but abandoned me to follow.

Oh no they did *not.*

Cursing again, arms crossed over my chest as I mumbled furiously to myself about boys and their arrogance, I stomped my bare-footed way after them.

chapter seven

The soft, shifting, sandy ground heated quickly, catching the warmth of the rising suns to the point I hopped an undignified, hissing gait punctuated with "ah!" and "ooh!" as the bottoms of my feet stung. Ram finally stopped with a heavy sigh, turning to glare at me while I dug my toes in and glared my fury.

Instead of commenting, though I was sure he wanted to from the irritated but amused look on his handsome (stop it right there, Sydlynn Hayle) face, he knelt at my feet with a murmured, "Your Highness." With two quick jabs of a sharp rock, he cut off two strips of fabric from each leg of my pajama pants.

My favorite pajama pants. He'd pay. Oh yes indeedy doodle. He'd pay.

Ram looked up at me, eyes twinkling. "If you would allow me?"

Like I had a choice. I lifted one red-tinted foot, wincing at the state of my black toenails, wondering if Ram thought they were ugly. Yeah, cut that thought off at the pass. Not that I was usually worried about a pedi, but demon toes weren't all that pretty to begin with and my ordeal so far had done a number on the hardened edges of my nails.

Vanity, Syd? At a time like this and for a guy deserving a butt whooping? Sad.

I instantly realized it was hard to stand on one foot with my arms crossed over my chest and, rather than hopping like an idiot, I reached out on impulse and rested one hand on the top of his head to keep my balance.

Hmm. His hair felt thick and very soft, falling in waves around his broad cheekbones, parting at his brow around his shining black half-turn horns, brushing his shoulders. He had it tucked casually behind one ear as his deft hands wrapped the flannel strip around my abused foot and tied it off.

Instantly better. But I wasn't letting him off the hook.

My other foot now protected like the first, Ram rose to face me, so close our noses almost touched. I was about to step back, but refused to give ground despite the fact my demon hummed softly to me she thought he had possibilities.

Traitor.

"You're welcome," he said. "Now, Princess, if you're

done whining, we have a way to go and, in case you hadn't noticed, it's not getting any cooler out here."

I forgave Quaid every single snarky thing he ever said to me and would have personally apologized to him in that moment if he'd been standing there. He had nothing on Rameranselot.

If only my demon kidnapper wasn't so creepalicious.

Muttering under my breath, eyes locked on the ruins of my pants, I snarled to my demon we would never, ever, even in the most desperate of moments even consider Ram as anything but a jackass.

I didn't look up until Ahmose sighed for the three thousandth time, a nasty insult barely held back between my clenched teeth, greeted by the sight of a low cluster of buildings emerging from the horizon.

"Finally," Ahmose said. "I was beginning to doubt you, Ram."

The taller demon wiped at his sweating brow, though his grin never faltered. "Faith, Ahmose. You lack faith."

Now that we were finally close to civilization, no matter how civil, my anger slid free enough I really noticed the heat.

"How much farther?" I pushed between the pair and stared at the town with one hand shielding my eyes from the dozen suns now beating down on us. I'd been here twice before and had never noticed a drastic upswing in temperature like this.

"Not used to the heat, Princess?" I was going to shove Ram's grinning face in the sand and make him swallow some.

Grumble, mumble. "It's not this hot in Ostrogotho." Crap. Whining. I hated whining.

"Protections aren't as powerful here," Ram said, eyes scanning the landscape. "All our suns pack a heat punch we'd never survive without some kind of shielding. But those in charge," yeah, go ahead, rub it in like I was one of them, "deem outer plane demons unworthy of their full protection."

Well... that kind of pissed me off, too, actually. Way to care for your people, Ahbi.

Ram didn't comment at my silence, just offered me another grin. "We'll make it," Ram said. "Though the more talking we do, the slower we are. And I'd rather not end up carrying you, Princess, when you finally faint from the heat."

Jack. Ass. I turned on him, smiled my sweetest. And wrapped myself in a bubble of cool air.

"Oh, I'll be fine," I said, kicking myself for not thinking of such a strategy before, but oh so pleased to be able to rub my superiority in his face. "Keep up, would you?" I turned and waved at the staring pair. "I wouldn't want to have to carry you the rest of the way because you passed out from the heat."

Ha. Ha. Ha.

So awesome.

No way was I sharing my little cocoon of yummy coolness, fed by my water magic, though I admit there wasn't much water to draw from. Just enough I could chill it down and keep myself in reasonable comfort as I strode, now whistling happily to rub it in, while the dynamic duo panted and tried to keep up.

I slowed as I neared the first building, not because I wanted to, but because the sight of it was a little unnerving. I was used to the opulence of Ostrogotho, where even the lowest plane was well cared for. The closer I came to the house, if it was a house, on the far edge of the town, the more nervous I became.

What looked like thin sheets of some kind of extruded metal shuddered in a low breeze picking up across the sand, sending whirls of dust devils dancing across the flat landscape. The rattle of the tin-like walls echoed to me, patches of green and black scars staining the surface in bruises of what must have been Demoniconian rust. One window, hacked out of the sheet, rattled in its frame, thin slats barely holding the clouded material in place. No fancy shielding here to keep nature at bay. Scrub greens, more brown than anything, clung to the base of the wall, hugging it as if for protection from the elements. I glanced over my shoulder at Ram who scowled, but not at me.

"Let me lead," he said, without a trace of snark, so I

allowed it, not sure what we were walking into. Though it seemed he did. Ahmose's wrinkled nose and disgust snapped at my temper for some reason, though I chose to ignore him instead of figuring out why.

I so had to get out of here.

Ram was almost to the corner of the first house, stepping onto a flattened path that passed for a road when a demon shuffled fearfully out into the open to gape at us. He was smaller than most demons I'd seen, narrow in the shoulder, bow-legged, clothed in sack-like fabric, feet bare and thick-soled. His amber eyes barely flickered with power as he slunk back from Ram as though wishing he'd stayed inside after all.

"We won't harm you." Ram's voice reached me as he held out one hand to the cowering demon. "We only need assistance."

Just when I was learning to despise him, he shocked me. Empathy poured from him, magic touching the other demon, supporting him until the frightened male bobbed his head in a welcoming nod.

"Pasht," he said. Grunted. I think he said "Pasht".

"Ram." The demon bowed to Pasht before turning to Ahmose and I. "Ahm," he said. "And Syd."

Pasht licked his thick lips when he looked at me, eyes widening. "Pretty," he said.

"She is, indeed," Ram said, shaking his head at me with a little frown as though to warn me not to respond badly. As if I would. So some poor low-plane demon thought I was pretty.

Hang on. Ram said I was, too.

No. No. No. No. Ram bad. No, Syd. Sheesh.

Movement behind Pasht's shoulder drew my attention as a round demon woman with hair to her hips and harsh-edged horns peeked around the corner, a pair of naked children, one boy and one girl, clung to her legs and stared with open mouths.

"What?" She said more than that, but it was hard to make out, some kind of guttural dialect I didn't recognize. But "what" was the gist.

Pasht spun and snarled at her, waving for her to go. She cowered back, burst into furious tears and screamed something at him that had to be a curse before she shoved her two now-sobbing kids back the way they'd come.

Mate and kids out of the way, Pasht gestured for us to follow him. I did so with great reluctance, keeping my magic tight around me despite Ram's seeming calm. Ahmose, I noticed, stuck close to me and I couldn't help but label him a coward.

I had no idea what to expect from this community of low-plane demons, though as we progressed past Pasht's house and moved deeper into the town, my impressions of their living conditions didn't improve. One dingy and half-collapsing house after another flanked the packed dirt street, a mish-mash of alleyways with openly running refuse and filth, narrow trenches dug between walls, coursing away from the center of the town. I remained grateful for my protective bubble and, from the look on Ahmose's face, I wouldn't be letting it down anytime soon. Not with him lifting the collar of his shirt to breathe through.

The smell had to be epic. Thank the elements for magic.

We began to gather a little parade behind us, demons emerging from their ramshackle homes with curiosity to drift along behind us, whispering and chattering, the sound growing as we finally reached what had to be the center of their little town, a circular empty patch with a hole dug in the middle. Rocks lined the edges, darkened with moisture as three demon women paused to stare, jugs of water perched on the lip.

A well. And while I knew my plane had people such as these who lived in conditions so desperate, I felt my heart go out to this community while my demon snarled and swore she'd do something to help them when all of this was over. Even though I knew from the echoing sigh of Ahbi's power, there was nothing to be done.

"Qesay!" Pasht stopped near the well and called out, focused on a rather elaborate version of his own home, decorated with colored glass and a few meager carvings and sculptures.

This will be their leader, Ram sent. *Stay quiet and don't insult him. We need their help.*

As if. As long as he didn't do anything to warrant it. I was not in the mood to be sold for a bushel of whatever passed for crops to these people.

I needn't have worried. The shuffling old demon who emerged from the house with one wizened hand gripping a warped staff for support lifted her head to stare at us, lips puckered, face a round, dried, dark red apple, amber eyes alive with magic. Curved horns spun in spirals by her ears, the most turns I'd ever seen on a demon, denoting great age. She held herself with immense dignity and immediately reminded me of Ahbi. So much so, I bowed my head to her. Eyes widening, she bowed hers in return, a little smile pulling at her mouth.

"Welcome," she said. "You come." Qesay then turned and shuffled her way back inside her house. I followed without fear, Ram at my side, Ahmose trailing, turning his head to look at the gathered crowd who pushed themselves through the door behind us until they blocked most of the light. The large hole in the ceiling, patched with multi-colored panes of glass, offered enough illumination to see the interior.

Dirt floor, a few rickety benches lining the walls and a large empty space in the middle. Had to be a meeting hall of some kind, doubling as Qesay's residence, a curtain of heavy fabric sectioning off one side.

I joined the leader in the center of the room while demons piled in after me, circling slowly, hunching down to wait and watch, mothers with babes clinging to them and older children pushing and shoving for a view, young male demons whispering among themselves while their female counterparts clung to each other as though we had arrived to take them hostage. A small group of equally aged demons, Qesay's peers I was guessing, came reluctantly forward. Three men and another woman joined Qesay, though held back from us while Ahmose waved his hand in front of his face.

"Damned low-plane stink," he hissed at Ram. "You'd think they'd at least keep themselves clean."

I spun on him as Qesay scowled and wrapped a rope of magic around his neck. The gathered village gasped as my power crushed his and drove him to his knees, his hands grasping at the amber restraint.

"Shut. Up." I turned to Qesay who was no longer scowling, but watched me carefully. "I apologize for our companion's insult," I said.

She stared at him while he writhed and snarled, holding herself still for a long moment, her people held captive by the spectacle, before waving her wrinkled hand at me, her black talons looking like stone. "Peace," she said.

I let Ahmose go, but not without a further shove, sending him sprawling as my magic released him. His magic rose to answer, but Ram's crackled once and Ahmose relented. The pure hate he shot at me through his amber gaze was enough to tell me I'd canceled out any good will I'd had with him, and sent him back to his original plan of having me killed.

We'd just see about that.

Besides, the grudging admiration on Ram's face was worth it.

Why did I want his approval again?

"You honor us," Ram said, bowing at the waist to Qesay and her council who tittered at the honor, considering they were of much lower status. "Thank you for welcoming us into your village."

Qesay looked back and forth between Ram and me, finally addressing me. I'm not sure what made her think I was the boss of our particular little group, except maybe she recognized a fellow leader when she met one. And I *was* the boss, yessiree. Ram would just have to suck up that particular bit of truth and choke on it.

"Honor to our *ghaman*."

Ghaman *means town*, Ram sent.

I got that, thanks, I shot back before smiling at Qesay. "The honor is ours."

"Lost?" Qesay's speech was longer than one word, but again I had trouble. I realized it wasn't a foreign tongue, but a bastardization of the language making her hard to understand. Good thing Ram knew a thing or two about being a bastard.

"We are," he answered her. "We need transport."

I almost laughed at him. The likelihood of these people having access to such advanced magic was so slim I expected them to offer us one of the flying dragon creatures I'd seen last time I was here. Come to think of it, I wasn't opposed to the idea. How cool would it be to fly into Ostrogotho on the back of a dragon?

But Qesay surprised me by nodding. "This way," she said as she turned and limped off, waving her staff with a growl, the circle parting to allow her passage, with us trailing along behind her.

Outside welcomed us, the brightness of the day forcing me to squint as I got used to it all over again. We didn't have far to go, though I winced as my flannel-wrapped feet slipped and landed in a trough of who knew what when I tried to hop over. Ram's lips twitched and I could feel the laugh building inside him through his touch as he took my hand and steadied me.

Go ahead. Laugh. Pay for it later.

Qesay gestured at a large pile of what looked like garbage, her magic humming softly around her. Nowhere near the strength of the demons I was familiar with, she had, from the way it felt, managed to maximize the use of what she did possess. Bits of debris and discarded junk flew from the pile, exposing a small and dented transport. Ram moved forward immediately with a smile on his face, but I winced. It was tiny, a personal vehicle, obviously, smaller by a quarter than the one Ahbi took us on to tour Demonicon. I glanced sideways at Ahmose who crossed his arms over his chest and scowled and I knew he was thinking what I was thinking.

No room for three.

Someone would be staying behind.

"I can work with this." Ram grinned at me before bowing again to Qesay. "Your price, honorable leader?"

I could see her mind working, shrewd eyes narrowed, a little grin on her face. "Power," she said.

Of course. It was the main currency of Demonicon, wasn't it? Even she wasn't immune to the call of more magic. I felt rather disappointed, though I hardly blamed her.

Until Ram nodded and held out his hand to her. Qesay shook her head and stepped back.

"All," she said.

Before he could act, I stepped up and held out my hand, my demon grumbling, but knowing what I was about to do was the right thing. "Our pleasure," I said, grinning suddenly, hope rising in me as I understood her request. She didn't want the magic just for herself. She wanted to help her whole village. And while the energy I could give them wouldn't elevate them far enough to do much good, I could at least make their lives a little easier by increasing what they could accomplish with magic.

I felt for Ahbi's presence, my demon's, joined it with the fire magic of my witchcraft for good measure and gathered a glowing ball of it, forming before me. Qesay's eyes flew wide, gasps making the rounds of her people as I turned to her and offered it up.

"For all," I said before focusing on the center of the power, even as I realized I had no idea what I was doing.

You do, my vampire sent. *Think of them as your coven. Share your power, leader.*

Right. Though I wasn't linked with them directly. So my job was a little harder. I reached out with my mind and found every single demon in the village, touching the tiny cores of magic they held inside. So small, so frail. That was about to change. Even my demon didn't protest at that point as I doubled my gift, feeling some of Ram's join me and, with a soft exhale, pushed the power outward to fill each of the villagers.

Qesay staggered, knuckles pink on her staff, but when she recovered she beamed at me, a gap showing missing front teeth. She fell to her knees, weeping, laughing, hugging herself and gazing up at me with adoration. I leaned down and took her hands, pulling her upright and handing her the staff.

"You're welcome," I said, feeling not at all diminished despite the fact I expected to, as the magic around me hummed happily in its new homes.

chapter eight

I'd never felt like a rock star before. But the adoration and sudden need of each and every soul in the village to come and touch me, fall at my feet in sobbing joy, was about as close as I could imagine. It wasn't until Qesay chased them off I was able to join Ram and Ahmose in their examination of the transport.

"You just wasted your power on them, you know." Ahmose's clear disdain made me feel I'd done the right thing even more.

"Mine to share," I shot back before turning on Ram, temper prickling. "Well?"

He straightened from peering over the rounded lip, a small console fading into the surrounding hull. "Well." He shrugged. "Nicely done."

"Whatever." I wasn't in the mood for platitudes. "Will it run?" I didn't like the idea of having to carry it with magic, or ourselves for that matter, any distance.

"I can fix it," he said, though dubiously. "There's enough residual power left in the console I should be able to get it running long enough to access sunlight."

"Solar powered?" How odd.

"Not exactly." He chuckled, leaned against the hull, grinning at me. "Forgive me, Princess. I keep forgetting you weren't raised on Demonicon. Fire magic. The ship should soak up enough heat to reactivate the core of fire magic. Then it's just a matter of giving it enough to wake the core. It should then begin to absorb what it needs to our next destination."

"Ostrogotho." I faced him down though Ahbi's power twisted suddenly in my gut in protest.

"Milanseme," Ram said. "We have a meeting we're probably already too late for."

"I don't recall agreeing to any meetings." What, stubborn? Me?

"We could knock you over the head and toss you in the back again," Ram said.

"Correction." I held up one finger, power sizzling down its length. "You could *try* to knock me out and toss me in the back. While dying. Slowly and painfully."

Ram shrugged. "Can you fly one of these, Princess?"

Oh. My. Swearword. His tone and the whole Princess thing was getting on my last nerve. "I can learn," I said.

"I'm sure." He stepped back. "Off you go, then."

The worst was Ahmose's smirk. The. Worst. He was lucky I didn't send him back in pieces to the city we'd left.

"Just fix it," I snapped, hating how easily Ram pushed my buttons.

"Yes, Your Highness," he said before turning his back on me.

Oooh. Creeporama.

I found a place to perch on a wobbling stack of something I didn't want to investigate closely, arms once more crossed over my chest, face set in a frown. I was going to give myself premature wrinkles at this rate.

Ahmose grumbled about the filth while both Ram and I ignored him. I found myself instead focusing on the rather shapely back end of the demon bent over the side of the transport, his shirt discarded, pants hanging low on his lean hips. A deep cleft ran between his shoulder blades, slight points of his demon's spine shoving against the skin, tracing a lovely valley down to his waist, disappearing under the fabric. Broad shoulders, gleaming with perspiration, flexed, muscular arms showing perfect definition as he used magic and sheer strength to lift the transport free and float it into the middle of the alley.

Yum.

No, not yum. Stop it.

But...

Sigh.

I shifted my focus to the narrow hull, several large

dents and one rather gaping hole in the side not adding to my optimism. But Ram grinned at me, turning so his muscular chest caught the light of the suns, bare and shapely, a thin line of black hair beginning at his sternum, tracing a line into his pants...

"Should be fine," he said as my gaze jerked from his waist to his eyes. Was that laughter?

Oh *hell* no.

"Better be," I said. Grumpy, yup, yup. "Just hurry up."

Ram bowed, winked. Flexed his chest.

Creepzilla.

I lurched to my feet and spun on my heel, marching to the end of the short alley, my back to them both. My demon might have been a traitor, oogling some guy who, admittedly, was rather attractive. Or would have been if he hadn't kidnapped me. But I wasn't about to fall for his charms, no way, no how.

The heat of the suns was finally starting to affect me, breaking through the surface of my water shield. I could only imagine how hot it was for the boys, but I chose heartless over helping. Forget it. They could fend for themselves. Since this was their fault.

Syd. I meeped a little cry of nerves as Sassafras's voice reached me, faint but there.

I glanced over my shoulder, but neither Ahmose nor Ram were looking my way. Ducking around the end of

66

the building for some privacy, I reached out to my demon cat with something akin to desperation.

Sass! I almost sobbed with relief to feel him in my head, though it was only now I understood how much strain I'd been under and that the silver Persian somehow meant rescue to me.

Syd, where are you? I could feel him pacing, tail twitching, though for some reason our connection was weak and only showed me flashing images of him.

I was kidnapped. I ran him through the scenario quickly, wrapping it up with my best guess at our location.

Sassy sighed when I finished. *Despite his unconventional means,* he sent, *this Rameranselot's reasoning is probably sound.*

Um, what?

You were attacked in your cell, correct? I agreed as Sass went on. *Then your life is in danger.*

How do I know he didn't set up the little show for my benefit? Anger bubbled, new resentment rising.

Because your kidnappers killed the three Guards, Sass sent. *And are now to be executed themselves.*

Wait a second. Despite the growing heat, I felt myself go cold. *They were alive when I was drugged.*

Then either your two friends killed them after you were unconscious, Sassy sent, *or someone else killed them.*

Sass, I sent. *There's more.* I filled him in on Ahbi's geas while Sass grumbled softly.

Your father told me about this, he sent. *Let me feel.*

67

I opened to Sass, and despite the weak connection, I felt it when he first touched on Ahbi's power and then the geas.

Why hasn't Dad tried to reach me? I bit my lower lip, feeling it tremble as anger gave way to desperation. How had I ended up in this disaster again?

He tried, Sass sent. *Meira's with me and she tried. I've been trying for hours. But I've only now broken through.*

Through what? I pushed harder, trying to strengthen the connection, feeling something in the way. Something that felt much like the wall between me and the veil.

I don't know, he sent. *But at least I've finally found you.*

The trial? I didn't have to ask.

The evidence my mother and others have brought is damning, Syd, he sent. *I won't lie to you. But if we can get you back here, let the tribunal feel the geas, they will know you didn't steal Ahbi's power, but were given it willingly.*

As soon as he spoke, my demon grandmother's magic protested. With a kick in the guts so hard I doubled over with a grunt of pain.

Syd! Sassy's panic tightened our link, if only for a moment. *What happened?*

Ahbi doesn't seem to agree with your plan, I sent. *Not even a little.*

He fell silent so long I worried I'd lost him. *I feared as much*, he sent at last. *The bossy old bitch.* Funny how he spoke with such affection despite his words. *How long do you have before you have to move on?*

Now that we were talking about it, I could feel the pull of the geas building inside me, the thrum of the dark promise I had no choice in making. *Not sure. A while.*

I'll come to you, he sent. I could feel him moving. *At least then I'll be able to stay in touch with your father.*

No, Sass. As much as I wanted him with me, if he was the only one I could reach through this weird blockage, I needed him with Dad. My escape route, if I was ever able to break the geas. *Just cover for me.* The anger I'd felt returned, but I realized then all of my irritation and frustration had nothing really to do with Ram or Ahmose or being kidnapped. *I have to find Ameline.*

You're certain it's her? Sassafras's magic flickered as the connection weakened.

I am. My hands clenched into fists at my sides as I stared with hatred at the horizon, knowing she was out there, somewhere. *I have no idea how she did it, but she's here, Sass. And she killed my grandmother.* How much of my anger was mine and how much was Ahbi's? I didn't know. Or care. Revenge it was.

I could feel Sass's hesitation, but he finally hugged me with his mind. *Be careful*, he sent. *And stay in close touch.* A little pause. *You can trust this Ram, Syd?*

I have no idea, I sent. *But I don't have much choice.*

He sadly broke contact while I sagged back against the side of the building, almost falling as the wobbly wall gave way. Ram appeared just as I staggered forward to prevent the catastrophic collapse of a villager's house. He caught me, pulling me upright.

Amber eyes studied me a moment. Did he know I had been talking to Sass? Was he or those he worked for the cause of the blockage keeping me from talking to my father or using the veil? And *could* I trust him?

Those questions swam around inside my head like starving sharks while Ram released me with a little smile.

"I fixed it, Princess," he said. "Time to go."

chapter nine

I followed Ram around the corner, unsurprised to find Ahmose standing between us and it.

"This transport is only big enough for two," he said, power crackling around him. "Which takes us back to my original idea, Ram."

"I suppose it does," Ram said, tone casual though his body was tense, shoulders pulling against his shirt as he stepped in front of me. "But somehow I don't think the princess will go willingly."

I shoved him aside, glaring at Ahmose as my own magic swelled. I let it all out, filling the filthy alley with the full power I had in my possession. Green Sidhe magic pooled along the ground, white vampire energy misting around me even as the family magic of the Hayle coven formed a small tornado at my back while fire crackled and my vision turned amber.

Ahmose paled, fell back a step. "Ram, do something."

"I plan on it," Ram said. Turned to me. "Unless you'd like to take care of it?"

"My pleasure." I didn't give Ahmose a moment to realize what we were talking about before I formed a multi-colored whip of magic and slashed him with it.

Ahmose fell back, landing on his civilized behind, scrambling to escape only to have Ram's magic form a wall behind him. I cracked my whip again, the air snapping with its speed, sparks falling over the fallen demon as Ram approached him, stopping only when he stood over the terrified Ahmose.

"There's only room for two," he said. "And you're off the list."

I felt what Ram was doing, pulled my own magic back as the demon stripped his fellow. But before I could stop him, cry out, not wishing such emptiness as I'd seen in Sassy's victim, Raneen, Ram pulled back, eyes blazing, power crackling over him while Ahmose sagged.

"You'll be executed for this," Ahmose said, voice a wheeze of exhaustion.

Ram laughed, deep and rumbling. "If you think this is the only thing I've done worthy of execution, you somehow missed the whole kidnapping a princess thing." Ram looked up and winked at me. I could feel the demon in him pulsing, eager, but the madness that took me when I drained Cypherion, the same madness Dad suffered when Ahbi forced him to fight and defeat Vandelarius, wasn't present. Which was a good thing. I didn't know, even with my advanced power, if I would have been able to control or contain Ram if that were the case.

Qesay appeared at the end of the alley, took one look at Ahmose and nodded quickly.

"Guards," she said, pointing to the east. How she knew who we were running from or that we were running at all I didn't know, but Ram grinned and kissed her cheek while she pinched his behind and smiled at me.

Qesay summoned a few of her people while Ram turned to the transport and touched the hull. All the power he'd taken from Ahmose flowed into the ship, returning Ram to his regular strength. He leaned back with a shake of his head and a rueful grin.

"I hope you appreciate this, Princess," he said.

"It's your hide you're saving." I was already climbing in the back, knowing it was crazy to trust him, but Ahbi's insistence at the thought of being caught and taken back to Ostrogotho drove me to act. "Now fly this thing already."

The hull hummed under me, seat forming to cup my body as Ram slid in the front, the console rising to his touch. I waved at Qesay while Pasht and two other men bound the weakly protesting Ahmose as the transport shuddered, bubble of shielding forming around us.

"They'll find you!" Ahmose's weak cry made it

through. "I told them where you were going."

"Idiot." Ram's hands clutched the controls. "He's a spy after all."

I clung to his waist, so close he pressed fully against me, as the transport rose above the little village. A quick look to the right revealed three large vehicles heading our way.

"Hang on," Ram said, before banking sharply and goosing the power.

Whether the slim, small hull made it more apparent or I'd never really gone this fast before, it didn't matter. We whipped through the sky as though thrown by a catapult, the village left far behind before I could even turn to look back. Ram swerved as I was turning around again, almost giving me whiplash.

"Watch it!" I squeezed his waist in protest.

"So you want to be caught?" Ram laughed, the sound filling the cabin. "I'll just slow down and let them reach us then." He finished with another swerve and I almost rewarded him with the bile in my stomach.

I bit back a response, but only because my eyes settled on the giant waterfall up ahead. I'd seen it before, on the little tour Ahbi gave us. We'd plunged through the beautiful mists, down through the clouds of moisture into the cavernous rent the water carved into the earth, frothing as pink as Kool Aid. And while my previous experience with this place had been breathtaking in its beauty, this one was proving to be more so.

For the wrong reasons.

"Are you insane?" I jabbed Ram in the ribs as he dove directly for the water, terror rising and taking my breath.

"Just trust me, Princess," he grunted, whole body tense, veins standing out on his corded neck and forearms as he battled the rising mist. The transport suddenly dropped fifty feet before rising quickly again, the entire hull vibrating from the pressure. The thermals and temperature changes in the air had to be immense. And while someone like Ahbi, with all the power of Demonicon at her disposal, handled it easily, I realized Ram didn't have her ability.

My magic joined his, forming a seamless bond as I reinforced the shielding and offered him better control. Our ride steadied immediately, smoothing out from the bucking, my insides slowly settling. I barely had time to wince and squeeze my eyes to slits before we passed through the thundering fall of water. The ship shuddered from the downpour as I held my breath for the inevitable impact with solid rock.

To my surprise, we emerged in a large cavern, tinted red from the water falling behind us. Ram slowly spun the transport and settled us on the ground, letting the shielding drop.

I recommend we both ward ourselves from being detected. His mental voice was barely loud enough for me to hear over the sound of the falls as he leaped out of the ship and stared at the water. I immediately shielded, pouring on the layers of defenses I'd perfected years ago, adding to them to block out Ahbi's power from those who sought us.

Ram quivered. *They're coming.*

I joined him, the falling water mesmerizing. His shields were strong, but not strong enough. I reached out to him, expanded mine, let witch and Sidhe, vampire and demon magic flow over him, finally drawing on the deepest part of me, my maji power, creating a seal no Guard would be able to break.

Ram turned and stared at me, his first flash of awe quickly masked by a grin. *This will do*, he sent.

Better, I sent back. *It's all I've got.*

We both felt the pressure on our joint shield, three minds joined together, searching, sniffing. But they passed over us as quickly as they landed, skipping away. I held my breath and the energy hiding us until Ram finally saluted the falls.

We have an appointment. He gestured to the ship. *And thanks to you, we just might make it after all.*

I wasn't sure that was good news, but I followed him to the transport, the pull of Ahbi's geas weakening. As long as Ram was going the way I needed to go I'd play along and be a good girl. But the moment our paths diverged, I was so dumping his ass. As cute as his ass was.

chapter ten

After a quick check with magic to make sure we were safe, Ram and I climbed back into the beat-up transport and flew back through the falls. Now we were properly supported and not on the run from Guards, I was able to enjoy the view more. Ram spun us sideways part way up the falls, mist sheeting over our shields, the thundering sound of falling water still so loud my teeth rattled together. But the sight was stunning. The elemental pressure of the red-tinted moisture shook the slim hull, vibration adding to the thrill of hovering in mid-air surrounded by primal power.

Speaking of primal power, my demon, now safe and off alert mode, was having more than a little fun with the whole Ram-in-my-lap situation. After I caught her sliding my fingers under the hem of his shirt, I forced my hands to my sides and clenched them into fists. If Ram had objections to either reaction, he had the good grace to keep it to his damned self.

Smart boy.

No beautiful dragons with multi-hued hides and massive wings graced the skies this trip and I found I missed the sight of them. Instead, as the largest of the suns set, leaving a few smaller ones to brighten the sky ahead, the sparkling spires of Milanseme beckoned.

"We have to use stealth," Ram said over his shoulder. "We haven't registered a flight plan and this vessel could be stolen."

"Nice of you to tell me now," I grumbled. "What do you want me to do?"

"Nothing," he said, a smirk in his voice. "But I wanted to warn you so you wouldn't fight me. I'm going to need control of the shields to make this work."

Shudder. He wanted control of my magic? Even my overly amorous demon side wasn't happy with the prospect.

Ram must have sensed my reluctance because his wide shoulders shrugged. "I leave it up to you, Princess," he said. "But there is no other way."

"I could do it." Big talk, Hayle.

"Perhaps," he said. "If we had time for me to teach you to fly. But I must manipulate our shields as I steer the transport. Both actions have to be in sync."

If he was jerking my chain, I'd kill him later. Sighing,

tension in every single muscle of my body making it harder, I opened my power to him and let him take the reins.

Tried to. Ram's touch was gentle but firm, kind but still foreign. My entire body twitched as my many sides fought him for control.

"Your Highness," he grated between clenched teeth as the transport wobbled in answer. "Perhaps using only one of your powers will do."

Ah. Right. I let him have my demon, since she was into him anyway. She grumbled at me, but complied, and, after a brief tango with Ram's magic, settled down to mope and let him take over.

It was weird, like being on autopilot, someone else manipulating my power. I wasn't sure I'd be able to repeat the performance if it weren't for my other magics. Though they also shivered at the thought of being taken over, the freedom of my vampire and Shaylee at least made the process tolerable.

One look out the window told me it wasn't working. "Um, Ram," I said, going for cool confidence while my heart tripled its speed. "That's a Guard transport."

He didn't answer, flying straight toward it. And its partner ship.

"Ram." I refrained from jabbing him in the ribs. "Ram."

The slim ship tipped, making me chirp a cry of

protest and grab onto him for dear life as we slid sideways between the two larger transports, clearing them as they hummed away without any indication they'd seen us.

"Nice trick," I said in his ear. "But a little warning next time."

His chuckle ignited my temper again, but I was in no position to do anything about it.

The last time I'd seen Milanseme, I'd been struck by the thought it resembled a very busy pincushion. Pointed, shining spires climbed into the air, the buildings all tall and slim, packed together, their roofs jabbing heavenward. The fading sunlight turned the horizon red as the last of the suns went down, an unhappy shade as the pointed city seemed to bleed the very sky.

"Pleasant looking place," I said, sarcasm returning as my stress level grew. I had no idea what was in store for me. This mysterious appointment Ram talked about had been so far from my thoughts I'd failed to ask any questions.

Yet.

"Like most demon cities," Ram said. "We're almost there."

"Mind telling me where 'there' is?" My stomach dipped in a quick heave as he dropped our elevation and scooted the damaged transport between buildings, skimming through the thin spaces. Now that we were in it, I shuddered at the thought of living in a city where it appeared most of the buildings had almost no living room.

Ram pointed as the transport dropped lower, heading to the outer rim of the other side of the city. I followed his finger, spotting a squat grouping of buildings, all porcupined together. He settled the transport in a dark alleyway, a gaping black hole at the end beckoning us onward. When the small ship finally settled at the side of a damaged building, Ram released his hold on my demon. I felt her sigh and stroke his power with hers before she retreated.

He'd better not get the wrong impression.

Ram turned sideways, glowing eyes meeting mine. Before I could offer a sharp response to what I could only expect would be some kind of snarky sexual comment, he nodded. "Well done. And thank you for trusting me."

"Wouldn't go that far," I said. "But my own personal safety is pretty important to me so, yeah. You're welcome."

Ram didn't say anything, just watched me with his steady gaze before releasing his shields completely and stepping out of the transport. He offered me a hand as I rose, stumbled, suddenly light-headed as my stomach complained and my mouth puckered with thirst.

"Don't suppose we could hit a fast food place on the way to wherever you're taking me?" A jolt of magic steadied me, but I'd have to have food and water eventually.

"I'm sorry," he said, genuine at last, real concern in his voice. "I'm sure my contacts will be able to feed us."

"The rebels." It was the first time I brought it up. "You work for the people who are against Ahbi and the ruling family." My grandmother's worries about the future of Demonicon came rushing back, tainted, I was sure, but the fact her magic now lived inside me.

"Your family." Ram paused before going on. "We only want equality for all demons," he said. "You saw how the villagers live." I couldn't argue with him there. Or could I? "Is that so wrong?"

"Maybe not," I said. "But there are other ways to go about it."

"I wish that were the case." His face shut down, cooled, jaw tight. I knew that face. The stubborn, rock-wall face. I'd worn it myself at times. But being hard-headed hadn't done me much good, and I was sure he'd run into the same trouble.

Not my problem. Ahbi's power suddenly hummed eagerly, the pull of the geas shuddering a moment before falling still. I could only take it as a good sign. Was Ameline in Milanseme? If so, this could all be over very quickly.

I was all for that.

"I promise, Leader will explain everything when we

see him." Ram's face stilled as his power reached out. He frowned after a moment, shook his head. "I can't get through." He grimaced, glared at me. "I've been having trouble reaching anyone since I met you, Princess. Your idea?"

"Not mine." I hated to admit my own weakness, but keeping the secret wasn't really serving anything. "I've been having trouble, too."

Ram grunted then shrugged. "I have to check in with the local rebellion cell. We're already late, so there's no guarantee Leader will still be available to meet us. But the cell leader should be able to tell us if we have a new contact time and place."

"Well, you go right ahead," I said, turning on my heel, feeling with my magic, with Ahbi's power, searching for the pull of Ameline. "I'll take care of my little problem first. Then, if I can, I'll meet up with you and this mysterious Leader of yours."

Ram's hand reached out, took my arm. Not a tight grasp, but a firm one.

"Please, Princess," he said. "Don't make me force you to come with me."

I turned back just so I could laugh in his face. Couldn't help it. Tears trickled down my cheeks as I giggled in near hysteria. Ram's expression flickered from confused to angry to tired before I ground to a snickering halt.

"It could be our objectives can go hand in hand." Smoothly diplomatic of him now he knew making me do anything would only get him in all kinds of hurt. "The rebels in this area would know if a strange demon appeared, especially one who might be stirring trouble."

Considering I was dressed in filthy pajama bottoms torn off at the knees, fabric for shoes and a grubby t-shirt that stank as bad as the rest of me, I was really low on options. I could have gone after Ameline, but would likely be arrested for vagrancy before I made it two blocks. If vagrancy was a crime here.

"Fine," I said. "But I'm starving and dirty and not in the mood to take crap from anyone. Fair warning."

He nodded quickly, smile returning. "The quicker we go, the faster we can both fulfill our duties."

So he thought of me as a duty. Okay then. So much for my demon's romantic interest.

Suited me just fine, thank you.

Before we even had a chance to head out, Ram froze, pulling me close from the grip he still had on my arm. A flood of demons melted from the darkness, at least a dozen of them, all staring at us with suspicion.

"Long live Ruler," Ram said softly.

The group relaxed as a unit, one stepping forward. She was a bulky demon, shoulders wider than Ram's, eyes too close together, a horn sheared off at her shaved scalp. A thin scar ran the length of her cheek, disappearing down her neck, corded muscles in her arms and bare legs intimidating.

"Luprimustica," she said, voice gruff and manly.

"Rameranselot," my companion said. "I have a meeting with Leader."

"Leader's gone." She stepped forward, eyeing me carefully, gaze narrowing. "You missed him."

Ram swore softly and shook his head. "He knew we were coming," he said. "Did he leave instructions?"

"No." She stopped just a few feet away, jaw bunching as she scowled. "Who's the girl?"

"The one who Leader wanted to meet," Ram said. "None of your business."

"It is my business," she snarled. "This is my territory." Lightning fast, she grabbed my opposite arm and jerked me out from behind Ram. Unprepared, I stumbled, almost falling to my knees, just catching myself. I surged upright despite the dizziness my action roused and faced her down. She was stocky, no taller than I was, but she had pounds on me I'd never match.

Good thing I had more magic than her.

Kinda than anyone, for that matter.

Her eyes flew wide as she stared before stepping back with horror on her face.

"Are you insane?" Luprimustica spun on Ram, fear turning to rage. "You brought her here?"

Ram tensed, pulled me back again while I snarled and

tugged myself free of his grip. "What do you know?"

"Only that her face is everywhere." The demon leader chopped the air with both hands. "And if any of us are caught with her, we're as good as stripped and dead." As her eyes settled on me again, Luprimustica's expression settled into grim fury. Ram must have sensed where things were going, because his power reached for mine just as the paranoid leader of the rebels gestured at me.

"Kill her," she said. "At once."

chapter eleven

I'd heard that before. And wasn't about to let some low-ranking rebel leader succeed where so many others had failed. Not when I was in full possession of my powers and able to defend myself.

It was almost comical their reactions to my sudden power flare, multi-hued magic rippling around me as I grinned, my demon's need to fight almost taking over. "Who's first?"

I wish I could say they turned coward and ran, not because I didn't want to fight or was afraid, but because I really didn't want to hurt anyone. Despite the fear on their faces, the bulk of the demons obeyed their orders and rushed me as a unit.

Only to fly back, tossed by a blast of air magic in a lovely arc, landing in a heap on top of Luprimustica.

"Nice technique," Ram snarled in my ear, hand

wrapped around my arm again, "but we don't have time to play."

I tried to pull free, but he had already turned and ran in the opposite direction, taking me with him. I could easily have fought him off, taken on all the rebels as far as that went. But the sound of a siren's screech behind us told me why he wanted to flee.

I guess I agreed with his motivations.

A glance over my shoulder showed Guards flooding the alley, the fallen demons struggling to rise and fight them off. One of the oversized soldiers spotted us and pointed our way just as Ram dragged me bodily around a corner and out of sight.

"Guards," I gasped as we ran, my hunger and thirst making it hard to drum up energy.

"No kidding," he shot back. "Your little display probably alerted most of the city."

Oops.

"Well, if you hadn't brought me into this stupid situation in the first place," I snapped as we rounded another corner and down a flight of stairs, "I wouldn't have been forced to fight."

"Shh!" He pinned me against the cold, stone wall at the bottom of the steps, an elaborately shaped metal railing above us offering a slim view of street level. Ram spun and snapped a tight crack of magic, shattering a round globe of magic hovering above us, plunging our hiding place into darkness just before booted feet pounded into view.

"Shield." Ram scowled at me. Like I needed the reminder. I stuck my tongue out at him, my wards already in place, tucking him inside as the first set of boots halted above us.

"Search this whole area." The deep Guard's voice reminded me of the sound of crushing glass. "I want those two rebels found."

Ram pressed me firmly into the wall with his whole body, lowering his face close to mine. "Close your eyes," he whispered. "They're glowing."

I did as I was told with a sharp remark ready to fire off, forced to hone it to a razor edge in my head, knowing talking—in this case, snarking—would make it more likely we were found. Instead, I clenched my jaw over and over as Ram's cheek settled against mine, my magic shielding us from the probing magic above.

It wasn't my intention to put you in danger. His mental voice hummed in my head, a bare whisper of sound. *I'm sorry.*

I'm sure you are. The slicing comment I'd been honing died a quick death as I softened. *Are you sure this rebellion you're part of is what you expected?*

He didn't comment for a moment as a second sweep of magic pressed against the shields, only to disappear again as the Guards moved on. In one way, their means of finding criminals was far better than normals at home. Magic as powerful as theirs could probably locate 99% of all they sought. But for a fugitive like me, they had no chance. In their arrogance, they moved on without a physical search.

Worked for me.

I felt the Guards pass us by at the same instant my demon purred and reached out her power to embrace Ram. His face turned, open mouth breathing hot air on my cheek, the warmth of his body suddenly acutely apparent as were the hard muscles under his clothes and the bubbling desire my demon welcomed and fed with her energy.

I caught myself as my head turned by her choice, Ram's lips hovering over mine, descending.

Perhaps another time, my vampire said. Dryly. Parching.

Both of my hands pressed firmly to Ram's chest and shoved him back as I snapped at my demon who retreated with a moan of frustration.

"If you don't mind," I said, proud of myself I kept my voice down, "we're a little busy without this kind of complication."

"You reached for me." Oh. My. Swearword. I hated his smirk. Wanted to claw it from his face. Was about to when I felt the touch of magic I knew. Not because I reached for it. But because the presence of it punched me in the stomach.

Gasping, feeling the desperate need and hate from Ahbi's power flare to life, I spun and looked out through the railing. At first, there was nothing, just a street with a few nervous pedestrians hurrying along, the odd slim transport.

When I spotted her, my entire body went rigid. Did I look that much like myself here? I didn't think so. However Ameline managed to take demon form, she still had the same face. I watched her cross the street with a young demon girl in tow, the child pulling weakly against her as though knowing it wouldn't do any good as the pair moved out of sight.

I scrambled up the stairs, searching for them again, while Ram hovered next to me.

"What is it?"

"The one I seek," I said, feeling Ahbi's spirit speak through me. "Stay out of my way."

I ran before he could answer, spotting Ameline and the girl rounding a corner two blocks away, putting on more speed, calling up Ahbi's power already hovering, ready and waiting to kill the girl who had murdered her.

Not thinking, hyper-focused on my quarry, I raced around the corner and right into a group of waiting Guards. They roared at me, magic lashing out to rebound from Ahbi's mighty power, sending them tumbling back. One look over their struggling bodies showed me Ameline, an angry smile on her demon face, the crying girl firmly in her grasp as she saluted me before running off.

My roar echoed from the walls, the surge of power taking over so strong I felt massive, as though I'd grown a hundred feet tall with muscles like a possessed body builder, ready to crush my opposition and go after her.

A flash of magic over my shoulder was enough of a distraction to snap me out of my delusion of goddessness. I turned to see Ram firing power at the Guards who were starting to recover. Grim and furious, his mind lashed against mine.

Another time and place. We have to leave!

I wasn't leaving. I had a job to do. Until the now-familiar squeal of a Guard siren warned me otherwise. More Guards were coming from up ahead. If I went after Ameline now, I'd be running straight into a battle I wasn't sure I could win.

Snarling in savage frustration, I whip-cracked a lash of power through the Guards before me, sending them screaming to the ground again, before spinning and following Ram out into the city.

chapter twelve

As we wove our way through the city, Ram moved with surety I wished I trusted. I fought off my demon grandmother's need to return to find Ameline and crush her like an insect. The pain was enough of a distraction I was grateful for Ram's guidance, following him almost blindly as my vampire, Shaylee and my own demon assisted my family magic in wrapping up Ahbi's insistence and smothering it before it left permanent damage.

I finally breathed a sigh of relief and came back to the outside world just as Ram pulled me to a halt in a shadowed overhang, cursing softly under his breath. I peered over his shoulder, realizing we'd circled back to where we'd left our transport only to find it under guard. But not by Guards. By a handful of nervous-looking demons who could only be rebels.

Ram backed into me and I took the hint, retreating a

few feet while he spun on me and drew me into his arms. Though the embrace seemed heated and passionate, the tension in his body as he bent over me told me this was subterfuge.

The only reason I didn't smack him.

His lips brushed my cheek as his mind touched mine. *We have to steal another.*

I could easily have blown through the ones hovering around our transport, but not quietly. *Fine with me*, I sent back, running my hands up his back as two people walked by, the female demon with her nose in the air while her companion whistled at us. Where had this willingness to break the law come from? Oh, yeah. It showed up right after I was framed for my grandmother's murder.

Criminal, it was.

Ram pulled away, but only a little, fingers wound through mine as he guided me across the street, free hand cupping my cheek, pulling me in to him, making it hard to walk straight.

Overdoing it a little, you think? The edge in my mental voice only made him grin.

Sorry, he sent back with a touch of magic stroking mine, *I thought you were enjoying yourself.*

Creeperino pigeramous.

And so, in full view of the other pedestrians, we sauntered up to a small transport and climbed inside. Ram didn't waste time, his power activating the control panel and we were quickly rising into the air in our new ride.

"You're pretty good at this," I said, offering up my shielding power once again as Ram turned to look back at me. Smirking again. Ass. Hat.

"I'm good at a lot of things," he said, energy reaching out to my demon again. He leaned back, pressing his shoulders against my chest, forcing me to lean into him if I wanted to keep my balance.

"Yeah, just so you know?" A shaft of magic from my vampire stabbed him in the kidney, making him cry out and jerk away. "Your romantic skills aren't one of them."

Darkness swathed the landscape as we flew free of Milanseme and moved on. I had to admit, the city was gorgeous at night, pinpricks of illumination glowing, the polished points shining in the multiple moonlight. But I was happy to leave it behind, especially when the throbbing pain still plaguing me no matter how much my other powers tried to protect me suddenly eased.

"Ameline's heading this way, too," I said without thinking.

"Then we have the same goals after all," Ram said. "You might want to thank me at some point."

Creepy creeping creeporilla.

Rather than answering with the smack to the back of the head I longed to deliver, I settled in my seat with my arms crossed over my chest so he couldn't repeat his little touchy-feely routine and stared out the bubble.

"I hope not all of the rebel commanders are like Luprimustica back there," I said, hoping to prod some information out of him. "Otherwise we're going to be in a bit of trouble trying to track down this Leader of yours."

I could tell by the twitch of his shoulders he agreed with me. "Each city has their own commander," he said, "autonomous, chosen from among those who wished to rebel. She was clearly an unfortunate choice."

He could say that again. "Best fighter wins, huh? Not a great way to pick a leader, Ram."

"No one said anything about fighting," he shot back over his shoulder. "You have a poor impression of us, Princess."

Oooh. There he was again with the "Princess" crap. I'd be shoving my Highness boot up his butt if he didn't quit it and see how princessy he found me then.

"Then how, smarty pants?" I prodded his kidney with one sharp index finger.

"By voting," he said.

I laughed. Couldn't help myself. The very idea of some kind of rebel election, held in secret, naturally, stirred up my sense of humor and images of cloak and dagger demons tripping over each other's egos.

Ram didn't comment, keeping his face forward, but from the look of the side of his jaw, I'd struck a very sensitive nerve.

I could have prodded him further, but it didn't seem worth it. Maybe when we were safely on the ground again.

I had to take my fun where I could get it, after all.

The rainforest on the other side of Milanseme glistened in the light of the low-hanging moons, canopy a black, glittering mat I was certain was thick enough to hold me if I fell. Not that I was willing to test it. The shining river winding through it ran pure silver, a ghostly trail bisecting the towering trees.

All thoughts of tormenting Ram disappeared when a flash of movement caught my attention. I pressed myself to the shield, grinning like a little kid as a pair of dragons, their multi-hued hides glowing softly, tumbled and danced, great wings spread.

"Hang on," Ram said, though there was joy in his voice. "We're about to have company."

Two more whipped past us, tossing the light transport as the backwash of their wing strokes buffeted our ride. I gasped in delight, laughing over their antics.

"How do they know we're here? I thought the shielding made us invisible." The impulse to leap out and onto the dragon's back was so strong I felt giddy.

"*Apparantelo* don't see or sense things the way we do," Ram said. "From what I remember of my studies, that is."

"Are they friendly?" Come on. What girl didn't want her very own dragon?

"In the air," Ram said as the same two who dive-bombed us dropped to hover near our shield.

I wasn't listening to him anymore. Not when a huge eye of dazzling diamond gazed back at me from behind the shield. I traced my fingers over the magic between us, my power reaching out to the creature on the other side. His power reached back, sourced in air and grounded in fire. His large wings fluttered, a slow blink registering his curiosity.

"I've never seen an *apparantelo* do this before." Ram's voice held as much awe as my heart.

"It's my air magic, maybe," I said, releasing a little more. The dragon—forget what Ram called him, he was a dragon, no doubt—did a barrel roll, calling out in a deep, thrumming voice, his song echoed by the female who rose to hover on his other side.

And then, in a flash of wings and staring eyes, we were surrounded, cocooned inside a flight of them as they matched our speed and trajectory perfectly. Ram's nerves made me laugh as I glanced at his turned head and caught the fear on his face.

"Don't worry," I said. "They won't hurt us."

"Says you," he said, but he relaxed a little.

My dragon—oh dear—blinked slowly again, craning his long neck around until his face was so close I could have touched it if the shield was open, wound his magic around me one more moment, the touch of him gentle but full of power.

Friend, he sent.

Before I could answer, shock taking my wits, the flight broke, dragons swooping away as one, gone as quickly as they'd come, diving for the trees and out of sight as their song rose and enveloped us, fading gently until it, too, was gone.

I wiped at tears I didn't know I was crying, unable to remove the smile wreathing my face.

"Holy," I said.

"Amazing," Ram agreed.

In silence, my heart full of something wonderful for once, we flew through the night toward our next destination.

chapter thirteen

Either the transport Ahbi used to give us our tour was much faster or Ram's magic just wasn't up to the same task, because it took us a couple of hours to reach Bilhaeder, just as the first of the suns was starting to come up. Nights were short on Demonicon, all those spinning stars making it almost impossible to predict, though I was sure there was a calendar of sunrises and sets somewhere.

Just as well. The view was even more spectacular than I remembered, the rainbow quality of the city's domes catching the early light, throwing back flashes of reds and blues and greens as we swooped low, still disguised by my power, into the edge of the city. I sighed sadly as Ram set us down on a quiet street, looking up at the tall domes further off, wanting to hold onto the wonder and contentment I'd felt through the ride, a welcome respite from the urgency of the last day or so.

Ram dropped his magic and I did the same, but he shook his head as he leaped out and turned to catch my eyes.

"I'm not risking you this time," he said. "Put the shields back up and stay here. I'll come back for you when I know if the local leader will listen to reason."

There went my good mood. "You're kidding me, right?"

Ram sighed, a fast, tight sound as his jaw clenched once. "Princess," he said, words honed to blades, "I realize you're used to getting what you want all the time—"

Snort. "You don't know anything about me," I shot back.

"—but I'm actually trying to keep you safe. Okay?" Ram's foot actually tapped on the ground as he waited for my answer. Was I getting to him?

Sweet. I shot him a girly smile and batted my lashes. "Yes, o brave and mighty warrior. Go save me. Please, please, save me."

His eyes narrowed, but he managed to keep his temper. Barely. The pulsing vein in his forehead told me I'd pushed his buttons. Wickedsauce.

"I'll be right back." He spun on one heel and marched off, disappearing through a door into a nearby building, the sound of the hissing seal opening and closing music to my ears.

The second he was gone, I dropped the shields and leaped out of the transport. Time to cut him loose and find Ameline so I could go the hell home.

And she was here, oh yes she was. I could feel her, thanks to Ahbi. The tug had grown stronger as we settled to the street, strong enough I knew if I let it lead me, I'd have my hands around her throat in no time.

One glance down at myself told me I would have to do something about my appearance, especially when passing pair of young demon girls giggled and pointed. I ducked down an oddly shaped alley, the two buildings bowing in toward each other and, as luck would have it, came across a clothesline hanging outside a doorway. A heavy black robe swayed in the breeze next to an embroidered dress and several pairs of undergarments I wasn't willing to examine. Guilt twinging inside me, I liberated the robe and slunk off as I pulled it over my head, a true criminal now.

The deep hood did wonders to hide my face, though the short bows and gestures passing pedestrians offered me made me nervous. My luck I'd taken the vestments of some demon priest or something. But no one seemed off put by the fact I was a girl or challenged me in the least so I smiled back and repeated their gesture as best I could.

Worked for me.

The tug of my grandmother's power led me several

blocks to a massive, domed building with writing etched in amber magic across the face. I had as yet to learn to read demon, but from the other black-robed citizens entering, it had to be a church or some kind of library.

Either way, I was dressed for the part. Confidence in every step I didn't feel on the inside, I strode with my head up across the street and through the large double doors into dim coolness.

Okay, so a cross between a church and a library. I was a good guesser. There were altar-like stands on either side of a massive entry, all glowing with power, rows upon rows of massive books just beyond. Above, floating on a transparent platform, were several demons dressed like me, etching words into the air as they chattered away at each other with great vigor.

University? A gong sounded and every demon turned and bowed to a large statue in the center of the room. I hastily joined them, shocked to discover I was genuflecting to my grandmother. The giant effigy rose majestically into the dome, standing, robed and holding a book the size of a transport in her hands. I felt a moment of regret, and sadness, as I gazed up at her face, feeling her inside me, and knowing, despite our differences, I'd miss her.

"May I help you, colleague?" I turned to find a small demon smiling at me, his thin horns barely turning a half crescent. Young then. And not very powerful.

"No, thank you," I said. "Just admiring Ruler."

He sighed, looked up at her, bowed. Wiped at one eye. "So tragic," he whispered. "You've heard?"

I nodded. Had I.

"I hope they burn her, the one who took our great Ruler from us." His tone had turned nasty, bitter. "She deserves the magma."

What was with burning people? I'd endured the risk of that at home, too. Shuddering, I shrugged to hide it.

"Things aren't always as they seem," I said. "Have a good day, colleague."

He bowed and moved on, though I noticed he glanced back at me over his shoulder and the look he gave me wasn't exactly friendly.

Goody. Syd's making friends again.

No time to waste. I continued to follow the pull of Ahbi's magic, growing stronger as I passed through the glowing, arched entry and into the library proper. I paced the rows of huge books, feeling the tug of Ahbi's urgency grow more insistent, until I eased around the end of a bookcase and spotted Ameline at last.

She stood before a large tome, open on the table before her, speaking to the girl she still clutched with one hand. The girl was weeping again, but quietly, as Ameline whispered to her. The girl shook her head, looked up at Ameline, whispered back. I watched Ameline shake her a little, felt the surge of her power as she did, knew from the fresh fall of the girl's tears Ameline had done more than shake her.

Enough. Time to act. Though I worried about the child and how I could protect her, Ahbi's geas had enough observing and fought me for control.

What is she looking for? My vampire broke through the pull and helped me regain composure.

Exactly, I sent. *I want her dead as much as the next geas, but her goal makes me nervous. We have no idea if she's already put something into motion that could cause us trouble later. I'd rather know for sure before I rip her heart out with my bare hands.*

An excellent plan, my vampire sent, *though I advise you do it in private. That much blood could draw unwanted attention.*

I shoved down a giggle, knowing my vampire didn't understand sarcasm and was being absolutely serious. Which made it even funnier.

I eased closer, head down, pretending to look at books while Ameline flipped a page and asked the girl another question. I was almost close enough to hear what she was whispering when she straightened and said in full voice, "Oh, there you are, Syd. How lovely of you to join us."

Ahbi's power shrieked at me to pounce, barely restrained as I closed the distance between us in a few strides, the table between us. Ameline was as stunning as usual, though her icy eyes were amber like mine, skin a pale red, the palest I'd seen on a demon, perfectly curved horns as glossy as her hair. As much as I hated to admit it, she looked almost better as a demon.

Though I supposed it fit.

"Nice to see you too, Ameline," I said with a vicious smile. "Time to die."

She didn't really look all that happy to see me, despite her words, frustration creasing her angry face. But she forced a throaty laugh, the girl beside her quivering as she stared at me in terror. "Don't be silly," she said. "I have far too much to do yet."

"That's what you think." I gestured at the book in front of her. "What are you looking for?"

"You'll see." Ameline winked one eye very slowly. "But for now, you'll have to wait."

"I'm done waiting." Ahbi's voice broke out of me as she seized my vocal chords. "I owe you a death, girl."

Ahbi writhed for control, but my vampire was right. If I was going to kill Ameline, it had to be somewhere less likely to draw attention and a gazillion Guards.

"Let's take this somewhere we can talk," I snarled. "And you can bleed without making a mess."

"I think you have something else to worry about right now," Ameline said.

It was only then I caught the flicker of movement and glanced around, noticing at last I'd been quietly surrounded. Black-robed demons crowded us, cutting me off from Ameline as she smirked and turned to a young male who made an odd gesture with one hand. Ameline repeated the gesture and pointed at me.

"As I told you, Fenukamadi," she said, voice smooth as butter and sweet as a candy apple from her very red lips, "the fugitive, now in your hands. Leader will be pleased."

"Well done," Fenukamadi said. "Can we assist you with your quest, colleague?"

"Not at all," she said with a smile to me. "You already have."

And while the pack of rebels disguised as scholars closed in around me, Ameline left, the girl held tight by one hand, waving with the other.

chapter fourteen

I could have let my grandmother's power out and attacked them to get to Ameline. Easily. Effortlessly. But doing so would have hurt and possibly killed a number of innocent demons and I just couldn't bring myself to do it.

Damn my conscience anyway.

Instead, Ahbi's power punishing me with jabbing pains to my gut, I turned and willingly went with the group now leading me out of the populated library and to the back of the room where I was funneled through a small door and into a private study chamber.

Empty, naturally. Perfect. Since I didn't for a second consider any of these demons innocent, I could act with impunity.

"We've been looking for you." Fenukamadi glared at me, gesturing to his people to guard the room.

"How lovely you found me then," I said. "But if you

don't mind, I have a sociopathic murderer to hunt down, and now that you've let her go, I'll have to chase her again." I closed the distance between us in two quick strides before anyone could stop me, my anger snapping on like a light switch as I jabbed him in the chest with my index finger. "Nice going."

Hands tried to grab me, pull me away, but Ahbi was pissed. Did I say pissed? She was so flipping mad, the moment the Grabby McGrabbers latched on, they were flung back, a giant shock of discharged energy sending them flying.

Fenukamadi vibrated with a mix of anger and terror, holding his ground.

"Ameline is one of us," he said.

"Oh, because she knew your stupid secret handshake?" I made a rude gesture with my middle finger. "How's that? Work for you?"

His mouth opened and closed once before he stepped back. "You're wanted by the Guards for the murder of Ruler," he snapped, the distance giving him backbone. "And by Leader for the same reason."

"You can tell this Leader of yours my grandmother was murdered, all right, but the one who did the murdering just walked out dragging a little girl behind her. And you let her go." I wanted to slam him with magic, my demon and Ahbi offering up the power to do it, but shoved them both back. "How much of a moron are you?

Didn't you think it rather convenient? Question? Second-guess?" He blanched as I went on, magic cutting through my words to slice the air. "Did you even for a second stop to ask yourself why a strange demon you'd never seen before offered me on a silver platter with no desire to take the credit for herself?"

"Colleague Ameline is on an important mission for Leader." Weak, so weak, his words, his tone. And even he winced when he was done.

"What mission is that?" I prodded him with two sharp points of energy, making him flinch. "Mind telling me?"

He stared, mute a moment. "She said it was secret," he whispered.

Idiot. Holy.

His shoulders squared as he drew a breath, clearly making up his mind to stand his ground. Double idiot. "We'll let Leader sort it out," Fenukamadi said with a measure of authority. "Bring her."

No one moved to touch me, the previously affected demons just regaining their feet.

I smirked, thinking of Ram. "You need an army," I said. "Got one?"

I had no idea what he was about to say, but it was the last real prod I managed to dig in. The door behind me whispered open, closing again quickly as the demon before me paled and bowed his head.

110

"Leader Culectorion," he said. "We've captured the fugitive."

I spun and glared at the new arrival, only to find Ram glaring back.

"I thought I told you to stay with the transport." His words spit out through gritted teeth.

"The last I checked, I'm the boss of me," I snarled back. Met the eyes of the demon beside him. No way this was big-shot Leader, at least not from his look. He seemed troubled, short and portly, reminding me a bit of Sassy's dad, Theridialis, though not aggressive at all.

"Your Highness," he bowed his head. "I'm afraid there's been a terrible misunderstanding. I've spoken to Rameranselot and believe we have a great deal to discuss."

I couldn't help shooting Ram a tight smile of disdain as I followed the small rebel leader, leaving the rest of them to trail in my wake like a procession.

I'd show them "Princess".

We wound our way through the building, down a steep flight of stairs and underground into a narrow tunnel. I didn't bother to talk to Ram who marched beside me, still seething, his magic pulsing in anger. Too bad for him. I had a job to do and if he didn't like it, he could suck it the hell up.

When we finally passed through a thick metal door and into what felt like an underground warehouse, I relented a little and reached for him.

Ameline was looking for something. His head turned just a little, a flicker of interest punctuating his anger. *I have to find out what it is.*

Ram shrugged, more to loosen the knots in his shoulders I was sure, because they settled more naturally as he nodded.

And then, there was nothing, nothing at all, but the heavenly smell of food. Hot and inviting, leading me by the nose to a low table with a cushioned bench where I collapsed and began to stuff my face while the demons around me watched in amazement.

I paused with my mouth full and met Culectorion's eyes. "Sorry," I mumbled. "Starving."

One of the demons lifted a steaming pitcher, hovering it over my cup, the scent of nectar so strong I felt the old addiction rise. But Ram covered my glass before the demon could pour and shook his head.

Outer plane nectar is stronger than what you're used to, he sent. *Trust me.* Pause. A sigh. *Why do I bother?*

Instead of shooting back a response, I reached for a second pitcher, this one gleaming with condensation, relieved to find it was water. Four big gulps emptied my first glass before I dove into the delicious food again.

Demoniconian cuisine had flavorings unrivaled on my plane, spices and sweetness I dreamed about. And while the spread before me had nothing on the banquets I'd enjoyed at the Seat, I thoroughly enjoyed every bite, even pausing to savor a few as my stomach expanded to uncomfortable.

Sighing in relief, sitting back with another glass of fresh water, I covered a little belch with one fist, blushing. I wasn't normally such a pig, but the combination of my demon's dominance and my absolute ravaging hunger had shoved me over the edge.

"Delicious," I said. "Thank you."

It made me feel a little better to notice Ram was helping himself pretty aggressively, too.

"It's our honor to have you here, Princess Sydlynhamitra." Culectorion sipped a cup of nectar while his people fell silent, eyes locked on him. While he didn't look like much, the impression was they respected and admired him. And since he was the first demon in this group of rebels to trust me—outside of Ram, I had to grudgingly admit—I leaned toward a bit of admiration myself.

"The honor is mine." I set my mug down, rubbing my fingers together to dry the moisture clinging to them. "I take it Ram has told you what he knows?"

"He has." Culectorion nodded slowly. "Might you fill in the rest?"

Encouraged by his attitude, I held nothing back, including Ameline's involvement and how she tricked my grandmother into opening the veil. The rebel leader didn't comment, though his people muttered occasionally as I went on. I finished with my encounter with Ameline and her subsequent trickery of his people.

"What could she have been looking for?" As much as the demon who'd collared me was still on my crap list, I felt bad for him, knowing how manipulative Ameline could be.

Culectorion shook his head, gaze far away. "I don't know, Your Highness," he said. "But if what you say is true, if this human disguised as a demon is a threat, we will find out."

"We're to meet with Leader," Ram spoke up. "We missed him in Milanseme because of our accident." Nice of him not to blame me, though I knew he implied it. Just knew it. "Is he in Bilhaeder?"

Culectorion shook his head, setting down his own glass, waving off the demon who tried to refill his cup. When his eyes met mine, they glowed amber, the nectar working its way through his system. "No," he said. "He's moved on to the next rally point in Ilogabon."

Ram swore softly, hands fisting on the tabletop. "I seem to be chasing his tail," he said.

Culectorion laughed, turning to Ram. "Leader is nothing if not elusive. And always on the move." He caught my eyes again, speculation in his gaze. "But he'll be most happy to meet you, Princess."

Culectorion swept to his feet, everyone else rising

with him. I grabbed a handful of nutty clusters tasting vaguely like chicken curry for the road as the rebel leader came forward to grip Ram's hand then bow to me.

"I will send a message ahead to Leader," he said, "to alert him you're on your way. In the meantime, I expect a bath and some fresh clothing will make you feel more comfortable?"

Oh boy, would it.

"Thank you," I said. "But I have one thing to do first."

chapter fifteen

Ram, now dressed as I was in a black robe, led me, a pair of rebel guards flanking us, back the way we came to the library and the table where Ameline had stood. The busybody colleagues already cleared the book she'd read from away, but after letting my demon sniff the spot, I followed her guidance to a nearby shelf and retrieved the tome in question.

It stank of Ameline, so much Ahbi's power jerked inside me.

Look, I sent, not knowing if what was left of her could understand me or not. *I'm doing my damned best. But if you keep doing crap like this, we won't get anywhere. Got me?*

The power fluttered, shot me one last jab and subsided.

Okay then.

Ram had already flipped the book open by the time I

finished my little internal argument and from the pale look on his face, it wasn't good news. Since I couldn't read what was written there, I had to impatiently poke him in the ribs to catch his attention. He was so concerned he didn't even frown at me.

"What?" I looked down at the sketch of what looked like a giant teardrop hovering in a cave. "What's that?"

"That," Ram said ever so softly, "is the Node, Sydlynhamitra."

The two rebels gasped, stepped away, also concerned. Not good, then.

"What's the Node?" I hated feeling stupid, but Ram didn't seem to find it strange I had no clue.

"You know our history?" He slid a chair out, sat down, hands shaking and I joined him, impulsively taking them in mine. "How we used to be multiple planes, all pulled together into one world?"

I nodded. "Thousands of years ago," I said. "Yeah, I know that part."

"Well," he said, "the Node is the core of demonic energy holding everything together."

Giant power source. Ameline. Yeah, this would end well.

"Ancient scientists created the Node as a focal point," Ram said. "Like balancing a plate on a pin. It keeps us spinning, linked. If the Node were to fail..." He shook his head, hands tightening around mine. "This Ameline of yours. Would she be so ambitious?"

Uh, hell yeah. And yet, no. If she was after demon power, why the center of all of it? Surely it would be easier to just take what she needed from other demons. Attacking a whole world? I didn't realize her goals had grown so big. "How hard would it be to disrupt the Node?" I had to find her. This could be a disaster. I couldn't even imagine the wreckage a collapse would cause, all the planes separating again.

"Not hard." He released my hands, color returning to his cheeks. "But she has no way of reaching it, Syd." I noted the lack of "Princess" and attitude. "It's impossible."

"Why, where is it?" I glanced at the picture again. "Underground?"

Ram closed the book with a thud. "No one knows," he said. "At least, no one but the monitors. And unless she can somehow find and coerce a monitor, she'll never find it."

"Don't look relieved," I said. "Ameline will find a way, trust me."

Ram's eyes locked on the book but he was far away. "This is terrible news," he said. "We're talking about the utter destruction of our race, Syd. If the planes separate..." He finally met my eyes. "The force of the destruction would wipe out most of the demon population."

"I'm not sure that's her aim." I chewed my bottom lip a moment. "The Ameline I know is evil personified, yes. But she claims she wants more power so she can fight who we both agree is a bigger enemy. And I'm not convinced destroying Demonicon is on her agenda." I sighed then and sat back, rubbing my aching temples. "Still, there's no question we have to stop her. Before she can get close enough to do any damage." Damn her, she was after more power, her insane need to become maji driving her still. Didn't she know by now stealing magic wasn't giving her what she needed?

"Hang on a sec," I said, confusion rising. "She already has demon power. She has to. Otherwise, how did she cross over?"

Ram didn't comment, watching me as my mind tried to wrap around the evil witch's motivations.

"Like I said, it makes no sense for her to destroy Demonicon." I tapped my fingertips on the table top. "So maybe she's just after a part of it." So many questions and no answers, not really.

"The Node is under delicate balance," Ram said. "Any shift in its output could mean the end. But it is constantly supervised. Demon monitors give up their entire existence to protect it and keep it stable, using their own power to do so, tied in to the Node so they don't disrupt anything."

"Would they be able to protect it from her if she did

manage to reach the Node?" It made sense the teardrop-shaped center of everything would have some kind of defense system. But would it be enough to keep Ameline in check?

Ram's shrug didn't make me feel any better. "The monitors themselves are the only ones who can access it," he said. "That's always been protection enough."

"All that power," I said. "And no demon has ever tried to steal it?"

He met my eyes with his brimming horror. "It would mean the deaths of all of us," he said in a shivering whisper. "Would you risk so much?"

I wouldn't. "Sorry," I said, not really meaning it. After all, this was Demonicon we were talking about. Power was the middle of every single driving emotion in the entire race.

Ram's fear didn't ease as much as he hid it behind a stubborn frown. "We need to warn Leader," he said. "And the monitors, if we can."

"And my Dad." Nice of him to leave my father out of the equation.

Ram didn't comment. "Regardless, if this Ameline wants to destroy us or if she only wants a fraction of the power for herself, the Node is just too fragile to tamper with. If someone were to tap into it, push it past their ability to keep things level, my world will be destroyed."

Right. Priorities. And happy thoughts.

CHAPTER SIXTEEN

Ram filled Culectorion in while I was led to a private room and allowed to collapse into a sunken tub carved from stone and soak the filth of the desert I'd walked through and the sweat of anxiety from my body. I knew I didn't have much time, but it was hard to drag myself from the water, now scrubbed clean and smelling of some kind of Demoniconian flower, toweling off with a soft sheet, dressing in boots—thank the elements. Boots!— flowing black pants and a tightly belted red tunic, tossing my poor t-shirt and what remained of my pajama bottoms in the corner. It felt weird to go without a bra, but I didn't have much choice, hoping my demon's larger chest, though perky, wouldn't bounce too much.

Making me blush. Because I thought of Ram and if he'd notice.

Aw, hell.

A metal ring with an elastic substance on the inside held my hair back and a warm black jacket hemmed at my knees finished the ensemble. Much more wearable than most of the clothes I'd been forced to choose from in Ostrogotho. If I saw one more spiked collar or platform shoe with blades and sparkles I'd kill someone with them.

By the time I emerged from my bath, Ram was on his own way out, almost colliding with me in the narrow, stone hallway. His eyes traveled down the front of my tunic, the open collar exposing a little more flesh than I was comfortable with, the barest smile on his lips.

"You clean up well," he said.

"Comments like that will get you a punch in the guts," I said, any flicker of attraction killed by his snark. I spun and stomped off in a huff, grateful for the heavy boots as I imagined grinding him under them with every step.

Culectorion waited for us at the end of the hallway, just inside the large, open area.

"Rameranselot has told me of his fears for the Node," he said, falling into step beside me as I crossed to the table and helped myself to slice of heavy, sweet bread, my hunger returning yet again. "And while I'm concerned, I believe this is something Leader needs to deal with personally." He snapped his fingers, a small force of rebels stepping forward and saluting by tapping two fingers to their left shoulders. "I've been in touch with him directly and he awaits you both in Ilogabon."

Finally. "Thank you, Culectorion," I said. "I appreciate the help."

"For now, we need to get the two of you out of here." A young demon handed me a sack with two straps and I could tell from the smell it was full of food. I winked at him as he giggled behind his hands and retreated before turning to follow Culectorion and Ram, our protection trailing behind us, to a far door. "A large group of Guards has just entered the city," the rebel leader said, hands clasped tightly behind him, "and I have my hands full protecting and hiding my own people. My soldiers will escort you directly to Leader and I ask you trust them as you would me."

I turned, caught Fenukamadi in the crowd and shrugged. "As long as they don't get in my way," I said.

Culectorion smiled as we paused by the door. "From the impression you've made, Your Highness, I doubt any of my people will cross you."

I hugged him impulsively, the bag of food hanging from one shoulder. "Thank you for everything," I said as I pulled away.

He stammered a moment before beaming at me. "Demonicon would be lucky to have you in Second Seat, Your Highness," he said. "Travel well and safely. Until we meet again."

As we followed the now-leading group of soldiers,

some remaining behind us as protection, I let the pull of Ahbi's power tell me what to do. Even though I was grateful, my appreciation for the food and the clean clothing genuine, this was the last time anyone would get between me and Ameline.

Lucky for the guards, I seemed to be heading in the right direction.

"Patience," Ram whispered as though sensing my intentions. "We'll meet with Leader and then deal with the threat of the false demon. I swear it."

"You can swear until your face turns into a rainbow, Ram," I said, "but if I see a chance to take Ameline out, I'm doing it. And your little rebellion be damned."

His face darkened, lips tight as he skipped a step in anger. "Is that what you think this is?" Amber fire glowed in his eyes. "Some 'little rebellion'?"

I glared back. "Let me tell you how much I care that you're mad at me right now."

Ram's shoulders jerked. "I'm struggling for the good of my race," he said.

"And I'm trying to ensure that race has a chance to reach whatever nirvana you're striving for," I snapped. "Or would you rather everyone died horribly when the whole show falls apart?"

Ram didn't answer. Not much to say.

Damned straight.

We entered a small hangar a few moments later, a

large transport, Guard in design, waiting for us. The soldiers jumped in, Ram offering me his hand though his face remained set in anger. I ignored his offer and leaped over, settling into a bench formed on the side of the hull, pulling my jacket around me, crossing my legs, letting my heavy boot bounce as my own temper simmered.

Ram sat next to me, soldiers lining both sides of the transport before two settled in magic-formed seats at the front. Power hummed to life, a bubble of shielding forming as we rose toward the ceiling. I looked up, watched the darkness crack open and part as large doors slid open, exposing the sky. Bright light made me squint as we emerged into daylight at the very edge of Bilhaeder and I was actually sad to see the shining domes disappear behind us, if only because they looked so beautiful in the sunlight.

And while I wanted to watch for the amazing elephant-like creatures I'd seen the last time I was here, house sized with what amounted to five feet and black hides, as soon as the soft rocking of the vehicle settled into quiet, I felt my head bobbing. I'd had no sleep in quite a while and more than enough scares, excitement and sadness to exhaust me. Stomach full, body clean and warm, I dosed in the quiet of the bubble of power while Shaylee sang a soft Sidhe song to me.

I have no idea how long I slept, but when I opened

my eyes, my cheek was pressed to something both strong and soft. I tipped my chin back and met Ram's glowing eyes. His anger was gone, arm around me, shoulder cradling me as I slept.

"Feel better?" He traced one finger down my jawline, thumb brushing my chin. My demon responded with lazy power, rumbling and purring, reaching for him as, in our drowsy comfort, he bent and pressed his lips to mine.

Demon. Kisses. Were. Amazing.

Amazing.

Fire power zinged over my skin and into my bloodstream, his magic heating the space between us as my demon sent sparks to him. His mouth tasted of sweetness, hot breath entering my lungs as I drew him close and let myself fall into the pure, primal joy of the kiss. Tingles ran from my toes to the tip of my nose, skin on fire, blood burning as it raced through my body, the connection between our power battling as much as caressing along the edges.

My hands dug into his hair, pulled him closer as he lifted me into his lap, teeth nipping my lower lip as we both came up for air. Not for long. Both of his strong hands pressed me tightly to him, one sliding under the back of my jacket and the hem of my tunic, flesh on flesh, the other cradling my head, pulling me tighter, the seal between our lips allowing nothing in but our breath, our fighting tongues, magic...

The soft bump of the transport snapped me out of my passion, broke the bond as I looked up, startled, to find we'd landed. The group of soldiers did their best not to grin, hiding their amusement behind their hands and in fake coughs as I glared around me. I smacked Ram's shoulder and slid from his lap, returning to my own seat, flushing so much my cheeks ached from it.

"Classy," I muttered, not sure if I was chastising Ram or myself.

"If Your Highness has finished," Fenukamadi said, eyes sparkling with amusement, "we've arrived at our destination."

chapter seventeen

I kicked my own sorry ass for the next several minutes while resolutely not meeting Ram's eyes. What was I thinking? This was serious business. Stupid romance and girly passion had no place in my mind. Or shouldn't have. I had a world to save, didn't I?

So why did I catch myself thinking about what Ram would look like with considerably less clothing on?

Syd. *Girl*friend. *Prio*rities.

At least our escort was over it, or at least had the good sense to stop with the smirking and sideways glances. They had to be all males, didn't they? I was surrounded by juveniles.

Time to get with the program. I steadfastly tuned out anything romantic and looked around to get my bearings. What I saw wasn't all that thrilling and almost disappointed me enough my demon's desire to think about Ram again nearly won.

While Milanseme was beautiful for its spiky spires and Bilhaeder stunning with its shining domes, Ilogabon bordered on ugly. All angles and odd shapes that made no sense, carved from the same red stone making up the landscape, it squatted like a bizarre growth punctuated by holes for doors and windows, reminiscent of rotten holes and cankerous disease.

I didn't have time to develop a hate-on for the place. We were only outside a moment before I was ushered through a dark red door, a few shades deeper than the building, and into cool dimness.

"Not far," our guide said as the soldiers formed up again, magic gathering as they prepared. "Just in case," he finished before we headed out.

Good advice. I called up my own power, just my demon's for now, feeling Ahbi's spirit answer, eager to move on. So Ameline had preceded us. More the better.

A short walk through dark halls, a quick street crossing and, finally, another descent underground and we entered a wide space, this one already occupied.

The waiting group of rebels were easily the largest demons I'd ever seen and I wondered if Ilogabon grew them bigger. Was this where the Guards were culled from, perhaps? But when Ram's shoulders twitched, I understood immediately, even before our escort formed up in panic.

"Ambush!" Fenukamadi attacked our opposition first, taking out a pair of Guards disguised as their own people before falling himself to a joint attack from the front line. More Guards rushed in, these in uniform, flooding the room while our group fell back. I whipped out my shielding, protecting all of us, feeling Ahbi's power protest.

Help, I sent. *Or screw off. Pick one.*

Her magic sighed and flooded forward, my air and earth magic connecting at the floor to seal us off.

"Back," I said through clenched teeth. "We have to retreat."

But there was no retreat, not with more Guards stomping toward us from the door we'd just exited.

"Now what?" I risked a glance at Ram whose eyes glowed and crackled with demon fire.

"Now, we fight." He flashed me a grin before howling his rage and attacking the Guards in front of us.

Fight I could manage. While the soldiers still standing backed me up, I let my power loose, not holding back any longer but unwilling to harm Dad's Guards just in case. I was already in enough trouble, thank you. So defensive magic it was.

Shaylee ripped her way through the stone floor, shattering rock with explosive power, sending Guards sprawling back. Yeah, not so defensive, I guess. But it was the only way I could make us room while my vampire chilled the air, forming a dense cloud of fog as my water magic sucked in all the moisture it could reach, air magic thickening and increasing the density until I could barely see Ram. I reached for his hand as flashes of amber fire flew blind through the magic mist, blocking the ability of the Guards to find us both with power and their eyes.

Come on. I jerked on Ram's hand, following the pull of Ahbi's geas, knowing she would lead me to an exit and escape if only so I could reach Ameline. My boot thudded against a doorsill just before my nose impacted the metal, saving me from injury. Though, from the shouting behind us, someone heard the sound, as much as it was muffled by the curling moisture in the air, and headed our way.

The door gave before me, not even bothering to search for a knob, blowing back under the pressure of my air magic. Ram and I staggered out into a long hallway, running immediately, still hand in hand. I looked back over my shoulder, spotting the shrunken band of rebels who'd escorted us chasing close behind, a group of Guards not long after them.

The hall ended in upward stairs, the sky calling us as we emerged into a busy morning street. Demons stepped aside in fear as we burst into the daylight and kept running.

"This way!" Ram tried to tug me off course, but I had my head and Ahbi's magic wasn't to be denied.

"Come with me or stay," I snarled, pulling my hand

free. "Pick one. But don't ever get in my way again."

Ram stared me down before nodding and running with me across the street.

I turned to the sound of shouting and a now-familiar siren's shill screech to see the rebels emerge and spin, attacking the Guards who fell back down the stairs, only to gain ground again. The battle quickly spilled out into the street, demons diving for cover or joining the fray, cries of, "Freedom!" echoing toward us as we raced three more blocks before Ahbi's pull jerked me off the main street and onto a crossway.

Panting, fairly certain we'd dodged another bullet, I forced myself to slow to a normal walk, gulping air. Five streets later, a small, open-air cafe offered a place to blend in as I slumped into a seat, Ram joining me.

"Have any money?" I raised one eyebrow. "I seem to be out and this looks like a good place to catch our breath."

He ordered us two drinks, as casual as if we'd not just been chased by Guards and narrowly escaped a battle I could still hear raging in the distance.

"How did they know we were coming?" Ram's face looked relaxed, pleasant even, but his words held venom.

"I have no idea," I answered, sipping the hot drink the young demon delivered after Ram handed her some small cubes of varying colors. "But I'm going to see if I can do something about it."

His brows drew together a moment, but I ignored him, the delightful taste of the best chocolate/mint/coffee/toffee I'd ever tasted on my tongue as I reached for the veil with all my strength and tried to touch Dad.

Nope. No luck. Whoever or whatever blocked me refused to budge. I tried Sassafras next, but even he wasn't accessible. While I ran through the list of people I could possibly try, a very weak voice spoke in my head.

Sydlynn? Is that you?

Theridialis. Awesome. I actually breathed a sigh of relief. *Where are you?*

Ilogabon, he sent. *Your father asked me to come, as part of the diplomatic team.* He sounded happy, delighted, even though his touch was barely there. *I'm so glad to hear you're all right. Your father is desperately worried about you. We all are.*

Did Sass talk to him? I had no idea if the connection would last, as it wavered and fluttered and wondered why Dad—it had to be Dad—was barricading the veil and how I could manage to break his hold.

He did, Theridialis sent. *We know you're innocent. But Sydlynn, you need to go back to the Seat. Are you still in Ostrogotho's borders?*

I wasn't sure why, but I immediately hesitated to tell him we were in the same city. Not because I didn't trust him. More out of wanting to limit interference. Maybe it was my grandmother's influence, but I smoothly bypassed his question with the best excuse I had. *If Ahbi's damned geas would let me*, I sent, *I'd consider it.*

Theridialis's mental nod was just discernible. *Leave it to Ruler to call on our oldest power*, he sent. *Have you yet been successful in your quest?*

Not really. I filled him in as fast as I could.

Oh my dear, he sent. *The rebels. Can you trust this young demon?*

Funny, your son asked me the same thing. I locked eyes with Ram as I answered, his steady gaze meeting mine before sweeping the street behind me. *I think so. He's had my back so far. Aside from the kidnapping.*

A minor infraction, Theridialis sent with his usual joviality.

Listen, I sent, *I need you to tell Dad to call off the Guards.* I filled him in on my worries about Ameline. Theridialis's mood shifted abruptly when I mentioned the Node.

The planes preserve us, he sent. *Sydlynn, this is terrible. That evil girl cannot reach the Node. The results could be catastrophic.*

No. Really? Sigh. *The more Dad puts pressure on me with these Guards everywhere, the harder it is for me to track Ameline.*

I understand, Theridialis sent. *I'll speak to your father as soon as I can.*

Are you having trouble reaching him? So it wasn't just me. But why would Dad cut off his own people?

Oddly, yes, Theridialis sent. *Usually mental communication is frowned on in Ostrogotho, but I have Ruler's permission to contact him. But I've encountered some strange resistance. As though the veil itself is rejecting me.*

Not just me. And maybe not Dad's fault after all. *So how do I find this Node? I'm tired of chasing Ameline. If I can get there first, maybe I can cut her off.*

Theridialis paused. *It's impossible*, he sent. *You had me worried a moment, Sydlynn. But in order for this girl to reach her goal, she must first be a Node monitor.*

I've heard that already. But if you knew Ameline the way I do, you'd know impossible just makes her want it more.

Again with a pause. *I'm telling you*, he sent, *she won't be able to find it.* A long sigh. *I was once a Node monitor. And I assure you, what she's considering would take a miracle.*

You were what? Ram's brows turned down in concern as my eyes flew wide, but I waved him off.

I wanted to dedicate myself to the Node, Theridialis said, some embarrassment in his tone, *but there are so many wonderful things on Demonicon requiring study. How could I choose?*

This is perfect. I caught myself rubbing my hands together while Ram gave me a funny look. *You can show me where the Node is.*

Silence. Long silence. *I can't*, Theridialis finally sent. *I won't.*

What the...? Seriously? *The fate of your world might hang in the balance here, Theridialis. In case you missed the point of this whole conversation.*

I promise you, he sent back, a hug just reaching my mind, *I will personally contact the lead monitor and warn him about Ameline. And I will talk to your father the moment I can. He's in the middle of his own fight, I fear.*

With who? Anxiety for Dad on top of everything else? Oh yeah. That was how I rolled.

The family, naturally. Theridialis sighed and sent me a soft touch, like a pat on the shoulder. *He's struggling to claim the throne, Sydlynn. Every Ruler does, but Haralthazar has an extra burden.*

Me. The mess. He didn't have to say it for me to know it was true.

A thought occurred to me even as my temper flared. *This was Ameline's goal all along*, I sent so sharply Theridialis pulled back. *She didn't kill Grandmother to hurt me, she did it to raise unrest. She needed a distraction to stir everyone up so she could act without someone figuring out what she was up to.*

Then I am very grateful you are on the task, Theridialis sent. *Be strong, my dear. The rebellion is only a short time away from affecting the entirety of Demonicon. Take care and I'll be in touch when I can.*

I broke contact, tossing down the last of the drink, but barely tasting it.

"Not good news, I take it," Ram said.

"Not good news." I thumped my mug down before climbing to my feet and offering him my hand. "If you'll trust me for once, it's time to go hunting."

chapter eighteen

I spent the remainder of the day with Ram in tow, following the pull of Ameline. There were several times we were forced to hide from approaching Guards and dodge fights still breaking out all over Ilogabon, simply blending in with the rest of the fleeing populace in most cases.

I had no idea what Ameline was up to, but she led me on a labyrinth chase all over the hideous city, and I began to wonder as the largest suns set if she'd somehow managed to trick Ahbi's power into following a false trail while our quarry eluded us and escaped.

Ram finally pulled me to a halt when yet another tug ended up in a dead end alley.

"Your method is getting us nowhere," he said, holding up his hands in defense as I spun on him with a snarl.

"You try following the geas of a dead demon Ruler," I snapped.

Ram bowed his head with a little smile. "I'm not faulting you, Princess," he said. "But something is clearly making our job harder. Might I suggest something?"

"Go ahead." I stomped one foot before crossing my arms over my chest, lips pulled down into a frown as my frustration grew. "But it better be good."

"No promises." He risked life and limb by sliding one arm around my waist and steering me out into the street again. "I have friends close by," he said. "Let's just check in and see if we can locate Leader. If not, we'll keep looking for your Ameline."

"She's not my Ameline," I said. "Fine, whatever. Except you're forgetting an important detail, Ram."

"I'm not," he said, eyes narrowing as his arm tightened around me. "I'm acutely aware someone has been alerting the Guards of our locations. Someone inside the rebellion."

"If you can't trust your people," I said, strolling with him as though we were a happy couple on a nice walk, "why are we contacting them?"

"We have no other options, in case *you've* forgotten." Ram led me by his grip down a set of stairs and to a door. Why was it always underground? The rebellion was taking the whole down-low thing a little far in my opinion. "Unless you'd rather go back to wandering aimlessly while your grandmother's spirit tries to narrow our choices?"

Grumble, snarl, sigh.

Instead of a rebel hideaway, Ram led me into what looked like a bar, the alluring scent of nectar and more delicious food in the air. I'd lost the bag of goodies I'd been given back in the ambush and my stomach was rumbling. Ram grinned, found us a seat in the corner, ordered dinner and disappeared, leaving me to pay with more of the cube coins. The server plucked a largish square from my palm with a wink and a smile, telling me immediately I'd been had, but it served Ram right for abandoning me. He rejoined me, winced when I handed him back his remaining money.

"You don't know Demonicon currency," he said.

"My, you're brilliant today," I answered sweetly. "Where's your friend?"

"He'll be along," Ram said as the server delivered our food. A quick flash of magic and a grim stare and his change magically appeared before him while the young demon boy flushed and trotted off.

"Bully," I said, helping myself to a bowl of green stew that looked horrid but smelled like turkey dinner and cranberries.

Ram just waggled his eyebrows at me, mouth full of a large chunk of pale pink bread.

We'd barely finished our meal, my body sighing in happiness as I sat back with fresh water to rinse it down when a handsome young demon slid through the growing crowd and approached our table with a wide smile. I watched him carefully, eyes scanning the low-ceilinged room as the noise grew louder with the addition of more patrons. Dim light kept the place intimate, the bar now packed with demons drinking nectar. I had a feeling we wouldn't want to be staying much past our present time, considering how quickly the gathering grew and consumed the addictive drink.

Bar fight pending, anyone?

Ram, meanwhile, embraced the arrival, slapping him heartily on the back before gesturing for him to join us. New boy had wide eyes, a jaw like a brick wall and a stocky build reminding me of a wrestler. Almost a head shorter than Ram, his friend's open, genuine smile had me smiling back.

"Syd," Ram said, "this is Mensahammel. Mensa, this is Syd."

Mensa bowed his head, still smiling. "Nice to meet you." He turned to Ram, grin fading a little. "I heard you were on duty in Ostrogotho. I take it something came up?"

Ram glanced at me. "You could say that," he said. "Can we go somewhere private?"

Mensa surged to his feet, all enthusiasm and happiness. "Come on," he said. "Mum will be happy to see you."

Before I could protest going home to meet his mother, Ram shook his head, though he stood as well. I copied him as Ram leaned close and whispered something in Mensa's ear. From the growing width of his eyes and the gaping expression he wore as he stared at me, skin paling, I figured Ram finally filled his friend in on who I was.

"Um, yes. Okay. Yes." Mensa bobbed another nod to me, almost bowed, caught himself as Ram grabbed his elbow.

Are you sure this is a good idea? I watched Mensa carefully as the boy practically stumbled over himself.

Just give him a minute, Ram snapped. *He's not used to this kind of thing.*

Nice to drop our mess on a friend's lap, I shot back.

He's the only one I know I can trust. Ram glared and I glared and Mensa stared so long I knew we'd draw attention if we didn't smarten up.

"Let's take a walk." I reached out and took Mensa's hand with what I hoped was a reassuring smile. "We have so much to talk about."

With Ram on one side and myself on the other, Mensa managed to move with some confidence back through the crowd and into the street. A small transport waited outside the door, which the young demon immediately approached. He flinched a little as he gestured to it. "I know somewhere," he whispered so loudly they would have heard him in the bar. "But we have to fly."

Ram patted him on the back. "We make do," he said, glowing eyes fixed on me.

Yeah. Two-seater. Just lovely.

I would have protested. Hell, left the two of them behind. But I had no choices. Ahbi's power grumbled, but the pull felt fractured, unfocused. With no way of tracking Ameline, knowing she'd done something to distort the geas, it was either trust Ram's friend or nothing.

And yet, that meant...

He'd better keep his hands to himself.

I sank into Ram's lap, turned sideways, unable to get comfortable until I wound my arm around his neck. Mensa took the controls in his nervous hands, the bubble of shielding popping in and out of stability a few times before he pulled himself together.

Is he safe to fly? My nerves had enough for one disaster, thanks.

He's the best pilot I know, Ram sent. *Just give him a break, all right? He's had a rough night.*

He's *had a rough night.* I kicked him solidly in the leg with the heel of my boot as Ram's left arm wound around my waist, his right hand settling in between my thighs. *Yours is about to get worse if you don't watch it, buddy.*

Ram's mental voice laughed. *We'll see about that,* he

sent.

A short trip later and we were soaring out of Ilogabon, heading for the grasslands beyond. The transport dipped low as, good to his word, Ram's friend expertly flew us close to the ground, skimming the tall stalks as we fled to the east and the darkening horizon.

"Not far now," Mensa said, cheery again.

"The pits, I take it?" Ram's arm tightened.

"Our regional leader decided to take advantage," Mensa said. "It's the perfect hiding place."

He's taking us to rebels? My whole body tensed.

I have to check in, Ram sent. *Don't worry.*

Right. I kicked him again with a scowl on my face, meeting his eyes with my own vision flaring amber as my demon rumbled her unhappiness. *So when the Guards show up, you'll still be telling me not to worry?*

For all we know, the traitor was in Culectorion's group, Ram sent, though he didn't sound completely convinced.

Comforting, I sent. *What are the pits, anyway?*

Old mining colony, he sent. *Abandoned for centuries. A maze only the miners understood. It's a great place to hide.*

But?

It's also a great place to get trapped.

Just. Lovely.

Too late to protest further, the little transport dipped suddenly, forcing me to grasp Ram's neck and hold on as we dove straight down. Mensa hummed a happy tune while we plunged into darkness.

In a sudden course change, the ship lurched, nose up, turning to the right, my body following, but my stomach slower to catch up. I gulped against my nausea as we took another fast turn in the pitch black, this time up and left.

"Here we go!" Mensa sounded so joyful I almost smacked him on the back of the head. I would have if I wasn't terrified hitting him would get us killed. One more solid plunge sent us plummeting toward dim, flickering lights. The transport's drop halted as the tail of it plunged to meet the nose, the vehicle coming to an abrupt almost halt, settling the last few feet as gently as a feather.

The shielding collapsed and Mensa leaped out, offering me his hand, grinning again. Demons emerged from the dimness, slowly, suspiciously, while Mensa said in his bright and happy voice, "Watch your step, Your Highness."

I glared at Ram who rolled his eyes and shrugged.

So much for anonymity, I sent.

Ram didn't answer, instead sliding his hands under me and hoisting me bodily out of the transport before exiting himself.

A tall female demon with double-curved horns and a grim expression marched to greet us. Her wide-set eyes flared a moment as she caught sight of Ram before they settled on me.

"Welcome home, Rameranselot," she said.

"Thank you, Leader Phineasoralo," he said.

"You've brought an unhappy guest." She tapped one foot on the floor, hands on her slim hips.

"We're looking for Leader," Ram said. "And don't wish to bring trouble to your branch."

She gestured for him to be quiet, shook her head. "Leader isn't in Ilogabon any longer," she said. "He's moved on to Nunaresh."

I knew that name. During our tour, my grandmother's aide Pagomaris cut our trip short, telling Ahbi Nunaresh required her attention.

"Another city," I said without thinking.

Phineasoralo fixed me with a sharp glare. "There is more to Demonicon than what your family controls, Your Highness," she said.

"Considering I don't live here," I snapped back, "I wouldn't know about that."

Her scowl deepened a moment before she nodded, relenting. "So I've heard." She glanced at Ram. "Since you're here, do you need anything?"

"Just a transport," he said. "I guess we're moving on."

A jerk from the pull made me wince. "I think Ameline's little trick has either worn off or we've cleared the influence of it." I pointed in the direction, off and up into the dark, though I had no idea which way it was.

"Nunaresh," Phineasoralo said. Hesitated. Nodded quickly. "Transport it is."

As she turned to take care of it, I felt a rush of disturbance in the air around me, my stomach clenching, a very bad feeling growing inside.

"Ram," I said, "something's coming."

I barely finished speaking when a siren sounded and all hell broke loose.

chapter Nineteen

Ram turned me around and shoved me toward Mensa's little vehicle before the fleet of Guard transports appeared from the darkness above. I vaguely heard Phineasoralo shouting orders at her people, thrown to the ground when a ball of blazing demon fire exploded on the other side of the slim ship's hull, cracking it in two and sending the pieces spinning like tops.

There went that idea. By the time I leaped to my feet, a shield firmly around me and, by physical association as he gripped my hand, Ram, two of the massive transports had already landed, Guards pouring out, magic flying.

This way! Ram's jerk on our mutual grip almost tore my arm from its socket as he dragged me like a sack of dead weight for the first few steps until I broke through my shock and followed under my own power. Mensa huffed behind us, too far for me to cover him with my shielding, though I did my best. Explosion after explosion rocked the docking area, small transports and large carriers owned by the rebels destroyed in magnificent showers of fire and sparks while the fourth Guard vehicle settled, dumping more soldiers into the fight.

I flinched at the glare as I watched the battle around me in flashes of amber magic, shadows of fighting rebels and Guards appearing back lit by glowing flames that burst into life before dying as fast as the next exploded.

It was impossible to tell from that point who was winning, how many Guard ships there were, how many Guards, even. Smoke choked me even as both Ram and I crouched low, Mensa on Ram's other side, running from wreckage to wreckage for cover. I jerked Ram back just in time, his hands grasping his friend, my shield vibrating with pressure, as a massive gob of fire burst in front of us.

We have to get out of here. I hated to state the obvious. My eyes roved the cavern, despairing at the loss of so many ships and my heart going out to the rebels despite everything. The Guards were crushing them, it was clear to me as I took a moment to watch a small detachment fall to the might of a group of hulking soldiers who pushed them back and finally sent them flying, limp dolls discarded in a blast of fire.

No formulaic challenges here. No taking of a sample of power as a reward. The Guards were stripping their opponents and using the magic against the rebels, not absorbing it as I expected, but balling up the liberated power and using it as weapons against its own people.

Ram's grim mind answered. *This is my fault*, he sent. *I should have listened to you.*

It's not, I sent back. *But regardless, we have to worry about it later.*

I know. He squeezed my hand as the floor under my feet rumbled and another massive explosion rocked the hanger. *I have a plan but you have to do exactly as I say.*

I nodded immediately and followed Ram and Mensa, the young demon wide-eyed and in shock, into the fight.

But not far. Just to the edge of the battle and around the back side of a landed Guard transport

My heart clenched as I understood. *Tell me you're not that crazy.*

It's our only chance, he sent. *Either come with me or stay here.*

Yeah, like staying is an option. Ram made a hopping gesture with his hand.

This won't work without a distraction. Mensa spun, face grim, tears tracking down his face. More sensitive than I expected. I reached out and took his hand as he punched Ram's shoulder before, bold and blushing, he kissed my cheek. *Be ready.*

Mensa! Ram reached for his friend, but he was already running off into the smoke.

I squeezed Ram's hand, empathy pouring through our connection.

He'll be okay. Liar, Syd. Pants on fire.

Ram nodded brusquely, jaw tight. *I'll fire it up*, he sent. *But you'll have to deal with the Guards Mensa doesn't handle.*

Done. Action I could manage. A fight? Just what I needed. We both heard the shout, Mensa's voice taunting the Guards. Ram and I peeked over the edge of the Guard ship hull, saw a small group of Guards rush from the transport, chasing Ram's friend back toward the fight, disappearing into the heavy smoke. One remained, hovering, focused on his departing friends.

My cue. I leaped over the edge of the transport, a little air magic boosting me up the five feet required to hop the tall side of the hull, landing softly in the middle of the Guard ship. The single soldier stood with his back to me, watching the fight. The small of his back bent awkwardly as my heavy boot landed with all the earth magic I could muster before he even realized we'd boarded. I'd intended to kick his ass off what was now my ship with that blow. Not send him flying twenty feet to crash into the backs of his fellow Guardsmen.

They spun as a group, Mensa's distraction broken, spotting me standing on their transport. Took them a minute to realize what happened, but the second they did, they ran for us, power lashing out. My shields whipped around their attacking magic, crushing it, but their second round almost made it through as I crouched behind the lip of the hull and shouted at Ram.

"Any time now, flyboy. They look a little pissed."

He laughed out loud, the shields of the transport humming to life to join mine as the third volley from the guards met both, striking sparks and throwing back chunks of flaming magic. The lead Guard tried to leap for us, hands catching on the edge of the shield as his fire magic burned a hold. But my vampire's spirit severed his connection while Ram pushed us into liftoff, driving me to my knees as the clinging parasite plummeted to the ground, crashing into his fellows, the fight below suddenly tiny, fiery.

Gone.

Up here, please.

I joined Ram immediately, taking a seat next to him at the front of the transport just as he banked us to the right.

"Remind me to kiss Mensa when I see him again." If I saw him again.

Ram ignored what I said in favor of focus.

"You know your way around the pits, I hope." Damn, I would have loved a seat belt.

"Enough," he said. "Just hang on. And be ready when I tell you."

"For what?"

"You'll see." He accelerated, taking the next turn so

fast I thought I left my skin behind.

I thought I was prepared for the climb, remembering the drop, but when it came, I had to clutch at the rounded dash of the transport as we literally flew like a stone from a slingshot up toward the sky.

The very busy sky. I opened my mouth to scream a warning as two Guard vessels crossed paths over the entrance, flinching violently as Ram steered us sideways, sliding between them with just enough room to spare. I looked back as he continued to rise, straight up toward the glowing moons.

"They're following." I gulped down my terror of heights, that one glance back a long and horrible look at how far we'd come.

"Not for long," he said. "Remember you agreed to do whatever I said?"

Oh. Hell. Gulp.

"I need you to hide us," he said. "But the timing has to be perfect."

"I can't make us invisible," I snapped, wound tight with tension as the air cleared, the thin rim of the atmosphere approaching. What was he doing?

"Just trust me. Please, Syd." I met Ram's eyes and nodded.

"Okay, ready? Ready... now!"

I expanded the shield around the transport, straining my power to cover the entire mass. This was no small personal vehicle, but a large hull designed to carry a hundred Guards. Ahbi's power blended perfectly with mine, clearly understanding if I died or was left incapacitated in any way, the geas would go unfulfilled. Just as I sealed the tail end of the wards, the ship rocked, an explosion buffeting our ship and sending us sideways before Ram got control again.

I spun on him, terror clutching my throat, making it almost impossible to scream.

Almost.

"WHAT THE HELL WAS THAT?"

"That," he said, smirking again, relaxing suddenly as the transport swerved, leveling out, heading for the ground again through a still-burning flare of fire, "was us dying a blazing death."

I stared at him, eyes flickering to the two Guard vessels that slowed as we passed them, ignoring us completely while Ram guided us away from the explosion.

"You're telling me I made us invisible." I looked down at my hands. Yup. Still there.

"It's the combo of magicks," he said. "I didn't believe it until I left you at the transport in Bilhaeder. When I turned to look back, it was as if you weren't there."

"You could have warned me. Told me. Something!" My insides quivered with retreating fear. "What was that explosion?"

"I had to let them get close enough to fire on us." We were close to the ground by now, cruising low despite our invisibility. "Nice job."

Nice... I was going to kill him the minute we were on the ground.

"So now what?" I reached out with Ahbi's power, feeling it there, but drained by the shield I still sustained. "It's pretty obvious your rebel friends are in trouble, Ram. And we're bringing it to them."

He nodded slowly. "Something is wrong," he said. "But we have to talk to Leader."

"From what we've gone through so far," I said, trying for concern and diplomacy, "if we do track down this Leader of yours, it's likely we'll be putting him in danger. And if this rebellion is that important to you, I don't think we should risk it."

Oh, Syd. Ulterior motives. But I had a job to do.

Ram didn't say anything for a long time. When he finally nodded, amber eyes meeting mine, there was sadness in his gaze.

"As much as I wish it were different," he said. "I think you're right. I can't figure out what's attracting the Guards. Neither of us is doing it on purpose."

"You think we've been tagged somehow?" That made sense, in a sick way.

"No," he said. "If that were true, we'd have been caught long before now."

"Someone in your group has access to all the rebellion's information," I said. "It's the only explanation. Do you have a way to communicate that doesn't involve mental connection?"

He looked at me funny, a frown bringing his brows together. "Of course we do," he said.

Right. Stupid question.

"That has to be it," I said.

Ram adjusted our heading, pointing to the twinkling lights in the distance, beckoning from the silvered darkness. "Nunaresh," he said. "Is Ameline there?"

A burning happiness filled me as I tested the pull.

"She is." This had to end. If only so I could get back to Ostrogotho, clear my name and help Dad put an end to the rebellion. As sad as it made me, no one would benefit from civil war. And considering the delicate balance the Node required, how would such a war affect it? I had no way of knowing and really didn't want to find out.

chapter twenty

Nunaresh approached at a rapid pace, the large transport's increased power traveling much faster than our smaller ride had been able to accomplish. I sat back and watched the tiny lights grow to towering buildings reminding me more of a human city than any of the others I'd visited here on Demonicon.

"Why isn't Nunaresh on the official tour?" I caught Ram's scowl before he answered.

"It's the only independent city on Demonicon," he said, voice level, but hands tightening on the sides of the control panel. That, paired with his frown, told me this was a major bone of contention for him. "The aristocracy can't be bothered with the lower plane cities, let alone one run by its own council. Your grandmother tried many times to coerce the rulers of Nunaresh to accept royal control, but she never convinced them and wasn't willing to start a war over it."

"I'm amazed she let it grow at all." The city fell away to my right as Ram banked around the outskirts. "Ahbi was such a control freak."

"By the time she discovered it had grown so big, it was too late to stop us without a fight," he said, bringing us in for a landing nowhere near the towering city center. "I don't know if you've noticed, but fighting is frowned on."

So much sarcasm. "You could have fooled me," I said.

"Really?" He released the control panel as we settled to the ground, turning to meet my eyes. "The formulaic challenge process isn't fighting, Syd. It's a theatrical joke meant to keep us in line and under control."

"Don't you think that's a good thing?" I shuddered a little, skin popping up gooseflesh as I remembered how I felt when I'd drained Cypherion. "Your race seems to get just a wee tad out of control when you're allowed to cut loose."

The bubble of shielding collapsed as Ram stood and offered me his hand. "Our race," he said softly as I rose to face him. "And yes, of course. You're right. But the days of barbarity are behind us. Our people stagnate, unable to grow, to evolve, because our true nature is suppressed."

"If I didn't think you'd all go up in flames," I said,

moving past him to the edge of the hull, "I'd agree with you, Ram. But even if you're right, if demons have developed past the need to fight for fighting's sake, all it would take is one to go a little too far and you'd have a monster on your hands." I turned back to him. "Trust me. I've been that monster."

Ram's shoulders twitched as he struggled internally. "We're not perfect," he said. "But we deserve the chance to find out for ourselves and not be regulated in every single thing we do by some Ruler who has only the advancement of her family in mind."

Wow. That was a slap in the face. Maybe I felt it more because I was carrying Ahbi around with me, but I doubted it.

"My family," I said with as much chill as I could manage, "has kept your people safe for generations. My grandmother," I ground the words out while my blood boiled, "gave up her entire life to guide and serve Demonicon." Definitely Ahbi talking, but I agreed with her. I'd grown up with the weight of responsibility on my shoulders. Ram had no freaking clue what that felt like. "And what did she get for it? Power?" I laughed in his face, bitter, harsh. "What good is that kind of power if you can't even be yourself, not even for five minutes?" Ram backed up as I advanced on him, one finger jabbing his chest as my anger rose, sparks flashing between us. "You think you can do a better job, smartass? You and your little rebellion with your Leader who just wants some of that power? Yeah, go ahead then." I turned from him, disgust rising like bile in my throat. "Good luck with that."

I hopped over the edge of the transport, refusing to look back, my fury cooling a little as I stomped my way toward the city. The soft thud of his landing and the crunch of boot falls behind me told me he was at least keeping pace. Not that I cared.

The more I thought about his excuse for the rebellion, the angrier I became. He reminded me of me when I was sixteen, fighting the system, unwilling to shoulder the load necessary to do what was right. Whining about it.

I had myself worked up into such a froth by the time I passed under an arched gateway and onto a long bridge leading to the city center, when Ram grabbed my arm I spun on him with my magic flashing.

He met my eyes, his calm, steady. Not challenging as I expected. Which cooled me off enough I didn't kill him.

For the time being.

"Let's find this false demon," he said. "We'll talk politics another time. Agreed?"

"Whatever." I punched him in the arm, the act enough to diffuse the rest of my temper, partly because I hit him hard enough he flinched. And grinned. Punched me back.

Tried to. My next punch would have landed him on his ass if we weren't interrupted.

Ram's eyes went flat, head bowing as I felt a hand fall on my shoulder, turning to find we'd been quietly surrounded. The rush of the water under our feet, running dark in the low light of the moons and my own preoccupation with my anger had been enough to distract me.

"Rebels, I take it." I glared at Ram who didn't answer. "You freaking turned us in again, didn't you?"

"Your Highness." A tall demon with a no-nonsense expression on his angular face bowed slightly to me, long hair swinging over one shoulder in a ponytail that hung to his ankles. "If you would please come with us, Leader would like a word with you."

I shrugged, threw my hands in the air. "Lovely. Fine. Okay. Great." Scowled at Ram. "Creep."

My lean escort ignored my last shot, one large hand gesturing for me to precede him. And while I knew I could escape him and his gang of rebels, doing their obvious best to look oh-so-casual and failing miserably, I figured once I met this Leader of theirs, they'd finally leave me alone.

And if the Guards showed up and kicked his ass? Not my problem.

I strode off at my fastest pace, unsurprised my escort kept up with me, though from the scrambling sounds of the foot falls behind we outpaced the others. At least the pull of Ameline's presence was still loud and clear. She was in Nunaresh, no doubt about it. And while I longed to run off and do my worst, I forced myself to be polite.

As polite as I could manage.

"Nice city you have here," I said to my escort.

"We like to think so," he answered in his low, soft voice, totally ignoring the peppering of sarcasm.

"I take it you have a name?" He almost floated beside me, a demon panther, expressionless but polite. I wondered how dangerous he was.

"I do," he said. "This way, Your Highness."

My, and friendly, too.

My tall guide escorted me to a platform where demons waited for a chance to catch one of the moving sheets of metal gliding between our point and the street across. A giant gap looked down over the next level of the city, and over the next, Nunaresh descending below into the underground while, as I looked up, it climbed in similar fashion above.

"How many demons live here?" I thought Ostrogotho was big. This place rivaled it in size, no question.

"Many million," my guide said, one hand reaching for me, not touching, just to encourage me as he stepped onto the floating rectangle, through the tingle of the protective shielding. The moving walkway sailed off in a smooth motion, without a breath of hesitation and though my brain screamed about the drop, I found the experience exhilarating.

"What plane designations does Nunaresh cover?" Pagomaris and Sassafras filled me in on the other four cities when I was here last. It was pretty easy from the almost circular design of the other places which level was which. Maybe the underground areas were lower ranked.

"None," my guide said with such coldness I looked up at him. His expression hadn't changed, hands clasped behind his back, but he continued in his same chill tone so I knew I'd offended him. "Nunaresh is a free city, Your Highness. We don't use status for gain here."

Interesting. "I didn't mean to hurt your feelings," I said. "I'm new to this, in case you didn't know."

His chin dipped, eyes meeting mine a moment, a tiny smile finally ghosting over his thin lips. "Forgive me, Princess Sydlynhamitra," he said. "We are proud of our autonomy here and will defend it to our last breath."

Ahbi's power hummed unhappily. Warning received and accepted.

We stepped from the pad and onto the next platform, heading west. I caught sight of Ram to my right out of the corner of my eye, still downcast, and started to forgive him. Maybe this wasn't such a bad idea. I might be able to help Dad's case as well. If I could talk the rebel leader down somehow, I could move on Ameline without so much disruption to deal with.

My guide paused at a tall and elegant house, the towering doorway already gaping open.

"Your Highness," he said. "After you."

Four stairs decorated with elaborate greenery and bluery and redery—seriously—led me up to the arched front door. I passed through, prepared for the worst, expecting to be drugged or attacked or something.

Paranoid? Who, me?

But when I entered the cool dimness of the interior, a large entry welcoming me inside, I instead found a small group of demons waiting. The front-runner stood huge and imposing, as big as Ahbi had been, with four turns to his horns and hair as silver as the jewelry he wore.

Why did he look familiar? The line of his jaw, the way he smiled, the width of his shoulders, how he carried himself... he spread his hands in greeting, closing the gap between us, coming to tower over me as I gaped up at him with a growing sense of realization rising to the surface.

"Sydlynhamitra," the demon who could only be Leader said. "I've been looking so forward to meeting you, my beautiful granddaughter."

CHAPTER TWENTY ONE

"My lord," my guide broke my gaping silence for me, "Her Highness must be ravenous."

Leader—my grandfather—nodded quickly and took my arm, linking it through his as he led me, unresisting, under a wide archway similar to the front door and into a long, narrow room, seating me himself in a massive chair before sitting beside me at the head of the table. My quiet guide gestured and the others in the room joined us, though I noticed he remained, silent and watchful, at my grandfather's shoulder.

"You seem surprised to see me, Sydlynhamitra." Leader—Grandfather—I'd heard his name before, hadn't I?

"I thought you were dead or something." Way to mumble yourself into embarrassment, Hayle.

Grandfather laughed, a deep belling sound, and his

followers joined him. All but his protector who held as still as ever. And Ram, beside me.

"Whoever told you I was dead? Your grandmother?" He shook his head, helping himself to a mug of nectar, which I rejected when he tried to fill my glass. "That would be like Ahbi."

Come to think of it, no one ever said what happened to Dad's father. And I'd not pushed the matter, either.

"Not her fault," I said, struggling with my composure as I met the eyes of the man who'd once ruled Demonicon with Ahbi. "I'm new around here."

He nodded slowly, the concerned elder, one large hand patting mine as he pulled his best loving granddad routine. He was so much like Ahbi I almost laughed, feeling the soft pressure of his magic, observing the polished way he performed for me. Wasn't buying it. But he didn't need to know that.

"I was delighted to hear you and your sister were finally able to return to your home plane," he said as a slim, young demon set a plate of food in front of me. I dug in, starving again, figuring if they planned to drug me they would have done it by now. "Though I am saddened by the circumstances of your homecoming."

"I bet," I said around a steaming mouthful of mushroom-shaped vegetables tasting of steak and maple syrup. "Having me kidnapped must have broken your heart."

The barest flicker of anger passed through his amber eyes. "I took the risk to your life much more seriously than your father," he said. "You have me to thank for your safety."

I sat back from my half-empty plate and glared at him. "No," I said. "Actually, if you took even a moment to find out anything at all about me, your little liberation act put your whole rebellion at risk." I leaned forward, letting my grandfather feel the edges of the power I had at my disposal as his eyes widened a fraction. "You have no idea who I am, Gramps. And I'm tired of your little foot soldiers getting in my way."

He sat back himself, a tight smile pulling against his lips. He really was a handsome old demon, my father reflected in his rugged face. "There are larger things at stake here, girl."

"You bet your red behind," I snapped. Guard boy wavered just a bit, eyes locked on me, but I ignored him. Just let him try anything and I'd have Shaylee's earth magic rearrange his body parts. "Like the safety of Demonicon."

"Your grandmother put our way of life at risk by perpetuating an unjust regime," Grandfather said.

"And was killed by an evil witch who wants to steal the power of your Node for herself," I shot back.

Well now. That got his attention. Grandfather paled slightly, breath catching as he leaned closer again. "What are you talking about?"

Before I could answer, a young female demon, the tiniest demon I'd ever seen, rushed into the room, eyes locking on me, a tall and stunningly beautiful female entering behind her.

"Henemordonin," the tiny demon said, hurrying toward us, as the wheels in my mind clicked over and my grandfather's name finally came back to me. "You promised you'd tell me when she arrived." The doll-like female stopped in a rush at my chair, barely taller than I was sitting as she stood there, beaming down at me, so much hope in her face, with her petite hands clasped to her chest, I lost my animosity and smiled hesitantly back.

"I am Avenesequoia," she said in her high-pitched but lovely girl voice. "Please," she went on, near to tears, lower lip trembling though she smiled, "can you tell me how my brother is? How is dear Sassafras?"

Sass had a sister? "He's fine," I said. Weak, Syd. Give her more than that. "He's here on Demonicon." In Ostrogotho. If she was a rebel, that wouldn't do much to help her.

But Avenesequoia beamed at me, leaning forward to kiss my cheek with her delicate lips before hugging me around the neck.

"Thank you," she said. "We'll talk of him later?"

I nodded as she let me go, turning to take a seat quickly vacated on the other side of my grandfather. Her companion slid into her own place, smiling at me with hooded eyes. Grandfather first patted the girl's hand, gazing at her with what seemed like real affection as she helped herself to a mug of nectar before nodding to the stunning demon next to her.

"Sekaniphestat," he said. "You've returned from Ostrogotho."

"Only briefly, my lord," the female said. "There is still much to do before our victory can be seized." She continued to smile at me. "Your forgiveness, Sydlynhamitra," Sekaniphestat said. "I was only acting on orders, you understand."

Sorry? "What orders?" I turned to my grandfather with a sick feeling in my stomach as I realized how much Avenesequoia, Sassy's sister, looked like the woman beside her.

"Mine," Grandfather said. "We had to get you out of Ostrogotho. And making you look guilty of Ahbi's murder facilitated that."

My eyes locked on Sekaniphestat as absolute rage flooded my body. Only sheer will power and my vampire's steady whispering kept me from flying over the table at the still-smiling demon.

"You're Theridialis's former mate," I said, proud through my haze of fury how level my voice was. "Sassy's mother." My demon squirmed for freedom, roaring for her blood. "You lied to the tribunal."

Grandfather squeezed my hand, drawing my attention. "As I said," he refused to let me go even when I applied pressure. "An unfortunate necessity. There was no way we'd be able to protect you in the higher levels of the Seat. We had to manipulate the facts to save you."

Such. A. Liar. "And destabilize Dad so he'd be in the perfect position to fall."

Grandfather had the good grace to flinch. Just a little bit. Only enough I saw it around his eyes, the tightness of his mouth. "Indeed," he said. "Now," he leaned forward, as though this revelation was nothing of any consequence. "Tell me about this threat you mentioned. The Node is in danger?"

Way to change the subject. I'd deal with the whole betrayal of all that was good and Sydly later. He seemed to be listening at last, a real frown on his face, so I shrugged and let it go.

"It's the reason I'm here in the first place," I said, diving into the story. He stopped me when I told him about finding Ahbi, skimming over her death as best I could. Grandfather—Henemordonin—needed more details.

After telling him what I remembered of Ahbi's death, I let him feel the geas she'd laid on me, watching his face crumple slightly, real grief clouding his eyes as his hand once again settled on mine.

"She was an incredible woman," he said. "Stubborn.

Self-righteous. Old fashioned and set in her ways. But I've never met anyone who I loved more than Ahbi Sanghamitra."

I caught the small scowl on Sekaniphestat's face, gone as quickly as it came at his words and wondered where her real loyalties lay.

I finished my story while my empathy grew for my grandfather in spite of myself, understanding he was who he was not by choice, but as a result of the pressure of his culture. By the time I finished off with what we'd learned of Ameline's goals and the warning of how we'd been tracked by Guards to every destination, Henemordonin seemed much more real to me than the mask he'd worn when we first met.

"Troubling indeed, my dear," he said while everyone watched him, including his protector. And me. I had to admit, he oozed charisma naturally, much like Ahbi , like my father did, only with the practiced ease of long centuries of use. "Though I have to agree with Theridialis of Fourth. The Node is inaccessible to those without monitor status."

Avenesequoia frowned into her cup as though wanting to disagree and I made a note to corner her the moment I had the chance. The furtive looks she cast my way told me I wouldn't have to force her to talk to me, at least.

"This rebellion has been brewing for centuries,"

Henemordonin said while his people sighed as one, nodding as though he spoke gospel. I scowled internally before forcing myself to listen and pay attention. If I was going to talk him down, I needed to understand as much as I could about his motivations. "I fought with your grandmother for what seemed like an age, but I always respected her." A slow wink, a bit of a smile, the benevolent Leader shone through before he went on. "But because of her refusal to accept other viewpoints, I have been forced to work behind the scenes, gathering to me those who are willing and able to free our people from her oppression."

Sounded like a well-practiced speech to me. "By starting a civil war."

Henemordonin nodded slowly, sadness returning, but the fake kind this time. He was demon enough, I was sure, to relish a real battle. "I have been prompting unrest since we broke our mating, shortly after your father was born. I gave up my position as Second Seat to work for my people's greater good." The watching demons were going to clap any second now. Seriously.

"Is it really worth it to start a war that will destroy all the good that's been done?" I was preaching to a deaf audience, I could tell almost immediately. Except for Ram, who hadn't touched a bite and watched me out of the corner of his eye, no one else paid the slightest attention to what I said.

"We will create even greater good, Sydlynhamitra," Henemordonin said with grand poise and a hearty smile for his followers, raising his glass. "It will come through fire and through hell, yes. But when we are through, all demons will be equal." Mugs thudded against the tabletop as they saluted him.

"What exactly are you aiming for?" Felt like communism to me. Not that I had anything against the idea. But it never worked out the way anyone intended. There were always those stronger and those weaker. Equality was a sad pipe dream.

Hey. I'd been paying attention in history after all. Wicked.

"Only what your own human people enjoy," my grandfather said. "I believe you call it democracy."

I had to laugh. Choked on it, flushing it back with a gulp of water while my memory teased me with Ram's mention of voting for city commanders. Was he really serious? "Demons won't survive democracy," I said. The very idea was ludicrous. What was he thinking? "You're going to rule by vote? Do you have any idea how many people would die every time there was an election?" I could see it now.

"We have no intention of lifting our laws against killing each other," Henemordonin said somewhat coldly. "But the status system serves no one any longer. No one but the aristocracy."

Such bullpucky. "You do realize cream rises to the top?" I looked around the table at the adoring faces of his followers. "There will always be leaders, rulers, in a way. Even in democracy, someone has to take the reins."

"Ah, but duly selected by their peers," Henemordonin said.

"Who've been brow beaten and brainwashed into believing what each of the candidates wants them to believe." This was a disaster waiting to happen. It barely worked for us on my plane. Put demons in a position where they could be led by popular vote?

Shudder.

"So you think a small family of so-called noble blood should continue to control all of our destinies?" My grandfather patted my hand with a disdainful expression. "You've been influenced by your position, my dear."

Anger stewed, churning in my stomach around the food I'd just eaten. "You fail to recall I wasn't raised on Demonicon." Temper, Syd. Diplomacy. "My position, as you call it, has brought me nothing but trouble." Story of my life. Deep breaths. "Have you even for a moment considered talking to Dad about this? He's not Ahbi, you know."

"I have great respect for Haralthazar," my grandfather said. "He resisted his mother far longer than any other demon has been able—myself included. But he is a son of the ruling class, sits in Ruler's seat. As much as

I love my son, he is now my enemy."

Talk about black and white.

"And even if he did listen," Henemordonin continued, "he is a young Ruler, not yet in control of his own family and position. While he might side with the rebellion, there is no promise the rest of Demonicon's ruling class will follow suit. No," he sighed as though in regret, the liar, "we've been complacent long enough. Though regrettable, your grandmother's passing is a sign we have to move, and quickly, to ensure we succeed in our goals for the future of all demons."

A murmur of agreement traveled the table, though Sassy's sister and Ram seemed to hold their peace, as did Henemordonin's protector.

Whatever. Let them implode, self-destruct. Dad had his hands full. But I had another job to do, one that would hopefully ensure he had the chance to kick his own father's ass.

I pushed my chair back and stood up. "Well, good luck with that." Protector demon tensed as my grandfather rose. A chorus of chairs scraping backward filled the silence as everyone else joined us on our feet. "Thanks for dinner and everything. Nice meeting you. But I have something to take care of and you, clearly, have plotting and mayhem to sort out." My eyes flickered from Henemordonin to his hovering demon attack cat and back. "Let me know how it turns out. Next family reunion."

"I'm afraid I'll have to insist on your company for a little longer, my dear." Henemordonin gestured, his lanky bodyguard coming forward instantly, power flowing under his taut skin and over long, lean muscle. "While you are my beloved granddaughter," yeah, right, "you are also the daughter of Ruler. Which means you are valuable in this beyond measure."

Oh he did *not* just call me a pawn in so many words.

"Belkni," he said, finally giving a name to the very dangerous demon I'd not once underestimated, "please escort my granddaughter to her new quarters."

CHAPTER TWENTY TWO

Good thing I was prepared for the worst. Had already begun to gather my power, calling on my healthy paranoia and the fact I was so used to walking around with my shields as a daily wardrobe choice I merely had to boost them with the magic I held in reserve, more than enough to block Belkni's slim, large hand from reaching me.

His power pressed against mine, not as a weight, but a slim blade, trying to slice through my wards and tear them open. I was ready for that, too, had read him like an open book, figured his quiet nature meant a more subtle style. I'd gone up against vampire Queens and Brotherhood sorcerers, demon princes and an Unseelie lord. And though I was well aware how dangerous my grandfather's bodyguard likely was, I was also confident he'd underestimated me.

I was so right. His edged attack failed, skittering over

the surface of my wards as I reached under him with my earth magic, Shaylee's green power surging forward to play and pinned him against the wall. Firmly. Not enough to crush anything vital, but hard enough I heard his head knock on stone.

They rushed me, almost as a group, Ram leaping to my rescue, trying to put himself in front of me, but he couldn't reach me either. And as the gathered demons summoned their own power, I showed them what I'd shown my grandfather.

They wanted scary bitch Syd? They could have her.

My shoulders spread wide as I grew in a rush, Ahbi's power showing me the way. The tornado of my family's magic burst around me, whipping my hair around, sending the table flying back, knocking some of the demons aside like a flat, rectangular bowling ball. It would have been funny if the other half of them hadn't thrown their power at me while Henemordonin stood back and watched, Sassy's sister looking desperately unhappy at his side.

Sekaniphestat staring with narrowed eyes, chewing her lower lip as though she'd made a terrible miscalculation.

The attacking magic I simply absorbed, sucking it into my shields to reinforce my power, a little vampire trick my demon happily adopted while she roared her fury at their nerve. I had no idea how powerful any of the gathered demons were, but their combined magic, while no real match for me, did pack a pretty good wallop.

Another swipe of earth magic rippled the ground and sent them tumbling, air magic pinning them to the walls, the ceiling, the crumpled floor.

"Enough!" I turned on Henemordonin and reached out with my power, scooping him up and dragging him forward, though his magic fought me as powerfully as Ahbi's aided me. If I only had her to help me, perhaps he would have succeeded. She knew him well enough, her magic familiar with his tactics she was able to pin him and hold him hostage, but it was the combined magicks of my vampire, Shaylee and the burning blue family power I possessed that put the fight to a very rapid end.

I didn't go so far as to force my grandfather to his knees. Humiliating him would get me nowhere. But I was done being pushed around, kidnapped, betrayed and bullied.

Done.

Henemordonin made a gesture at last, a cutting motion with one hand, and his people fell back. I expected fury from him, outrage. Instead, he laughed.

"Well done," he said. "Haralthazar has raised a most excellent child."

"Miriam Hayle raised me," I snarled. "And a coven of amazing witches." Bitterness toward Dad flooded me. Old anger I thought I'd dealt with already, but clearly hadn't. Maybe the fact he hadn't had the strength to free me in the first place when I was arrested for Ahbi's murder made things worse. Or facing down this arrogant ass who was *his* father. No matter the reason, I squeezed Henemordonin a little tighter before letting him go roughly, watching him stagger as I regained my normal size, shields still firmly in place and Belkni pinned to the wall like a roach. "And I'm no one's pawn."

Henemordonin's eyes narrowed as he caught himself, his gathered supporters still snapping with fury at how I treated their beloved Leader. Let them. I'd take them all on again, and gladly.

Definitely Ahbi talking.

"Leader, please listen." Avenesequoia clung to the large demon's arm, face twisted in upset. "You cannot win against such might. And Sydlynhamitra," she turned to me, "has proven she has our people's best interest at heart by going after a threat to our safety." She returned her gaze to him. "Our rebellion is already on the move. Surely we don't need to make an enemy of someone who could be a friend when we need her most?"

Clever girl. Too clever? Sassafras was brilliant, so it bore out his sister would be, too. But was she manipulating Henemordonin, or me?

Ah, cynicism and suspicion. My dear, dear friends.

"I believe this threat is as real as the war coming to our people," the little doll demon said. "And thanks to our former Ruler, Sydlynhamitra is the only one who can stop her."

"I also agree," Ram spoke up, the first words out of his mouth since the bridge. "Leader, I've been on this journey with her since I rescued," kidnapped, creeporama, get it right, "her from Ostrogotho. The Ameline she speaks of puts us all in danger." Ram took a step closer to my grandfather, head bowed. "Please allow her to finish her task while we focus on our freedom."

Henemordonin's eyes locked on mine. *You understand I had to try.* His mental voice was powerful, though the block in the veil made his words echo.

I'm not interested in your stupid rebellion, I shot back. *I owe Ameline for far more than killing Grandmother. So you damned well better get the hell out of my way or I will take interest. Capisce?*

Henemordonin nodded, ever so slightly before relaxing and smiling at me.

"Accept our gratitude for your vigilance," he said, motioning for the others to relent. Which they did, without question. That kind of unwavering loyalty made me very, very nervous.

My grandfather approached me slowly as I dropped my surface shielding and faced him down. One hand reached for mine, took it gently. "I am grateful for you," he said as he bent to kiss my cheek while I did my best not to shake my head at his arrogance. "Knowing I have such a fine, strong granddaughter makes my choices all worth it."

I bit back a sharp comment while Ahbi's power prodded me with a snarky comment. I could tell she loved him, but if he was this annoying most of the time, no wonder they didn't get along.

"I must oversee the movement," he said, backing away from me. Turning to look at his guard still pinned to the wall. Belkni didn't fight me, just hung there as though he belonged, eyes never leaving me, not an ounce of animosity present. "Your journey will be a dangerous one," Henemordonin said. "I must insist you take help with you, the best I can provide." Belkni's eyes finally showed emotion, flickering to my grandfather with a measure of surprise. "Go with Sydlynhamitra, my faithful one," he said. "Keep her safe as you would me, against all comers."

Great. Saddled with a sociopathic killing machine. Which, in all honesty, described Charlotte, my bodywere back home. Who would right now be going into apoplectic shock because of my absence if she wasn't deep in it already. So no big change there. Except this particular bodyguard wasn't on my payroll, so to speak.

I approached Belkni as my grandfather then swept from the room without a backward glance, Sekaniphestat at his side. She spared me one last look, though her dark humor had returned. I glared at her, hating her for Sassy's sake as well as my own, as my grandfather's entourage followed after him. Only Ram and Avenesequoia remained while I turned to stare up at the lean protector.

"My game, my rules." I tapped his chest with one finger. "First sign of trouble from you, you're entering orbit. Read me?"

He nodded, just able to move his head in Shaylee's grasp. "Leader has ordered me to protect you," he said in his quiet voice, "and I will do so with my life."

Lovely. I asked my Sidhe princess politely to let him down, knowing how much fun she was having and hugging her with thanks when she pouted over not being allowed to crush him to a pulp. I really had to have a chat with the personalities inside me. Their bloodthirsty natures were rubbing off on each other.

The bodyguard bowed to me as though he hadn't just been this close to death by squishing. "You asked me my name and, rudely, I didn't answer." As he straightened, he met my eyes. "I am Belkniatuman, but you may call me Belkni."

"Coolness," I said, turning on Ram. Pushing him hard with both hands on his chest so he staggered back. "You do that again," I said, still pissed, but not as angry as I had been, the residue of his betrayal enough to save his sorry hide, "and you're joining wonderdemon over here."

Ram nodded quickly, real regret on his face. "I'm sorry, Syd. I swear I didn't know he would try to keep you prisoner."

Avenesequoia snorted, grabbing my hand and tugging me away from the other two before hugging me with a fierce strength that made my ribs ache. "Idiots," she said. "But I knew you'd be well." She smiled suddenly. "He trained you to fight, didn't he, my dear Sassafras?"

I grinned back, unable to help myself. "He did," I said. "Has spent his whole life trying to whip me into shape."

Tears welled in her eyes as she linked arms with me and steered me toward the door. "You must tell me everything," she said, "while we search for this terrible infiltrator."

I had my suspicions about who the traitor's traitor might be, but kept silent. I pulled her to a halt while Ram and Belkni joined us at the exit to the room, realizing what she'd said. "I'm sorry?" I hadn't signed up for another passenger.

"I'm coming with you, naturally," she said. "Any friend of my brother's can't go into battle alone."

Oh boy.

I didn't resist as the tiny demon marched me out into the street, nor when Belkni escorted us deeper into the city while I literally followed my gut and the steady pull, though I told myself in no uncertain terms the second one of them screwed with me, I was dumping all of them over the side without a second thought.

chapter twenty three

I was just getting my bearings when a voice in my head brought me up short.

Syd! Meira's faint connection grew stronger by the second. Was she in Nunaresh? Why?

Meems. I grasped onto her, using Ahbi's power to boost the connection, reaching for my little sister with a desperation I hadn't known I was hiding. *Are you okay?*

Am I *okay?* She sounded exasperated, frustrated. Even a little angry. And though this whole thing wasn't my fault, I guess I couldn't blame her. *Where are you?*

Safe, I sent. *I'm chasing down Ameline.*

Theridialis told us, she sent, calming a little, the touch of her stronger than anyone else who'd made it through to me, though still tenuous compared to our usual reach. *But Syd, things are really bad here. Let Ameline try to get to the Node—she'll never make it. Dad needs us both here with him.*

Ostrogotho then. *Meems, you know I can't do that.* I drew a breath, trying to focus on the pull of the geas and my sister at the same time. *Not only do I owe Ameline for my own reasons, she killed Ahbi.*

My sister was quiet a moment. *They said you did it*, she sent.

Wow, how sobering. *And you believed them?* My own sister?

No, she sent, but there was hesitation in her denial. *It's just, you left home so fast and you didn't take me with you. And it was Grandmother calling. And you have her power now.* Meira wound down, panic and temper bubbling inside her. She didn't sound like herself at all. Was it just the strain? My typically level-headed young sister didn't often fly off like this. She'd been through as much as I had, thanks to coven life. But she'd never doubted me like this before.

I didn't hurt her, I sent, softly and slowly, letting Meira feel what she could through the block in the veil. *She came to me willingly and is forcing me to hunt Ameline. She wouldn't do that if it was my fault, Meems.* Though in the back of my mind, the niggling worry it was my fault, that I'd somehow left my grandmother vulnerable to Ameline despite the old demon's incredible power, ached like a rotten tooth.

I guess. Meira's mind seemed to drift a moment, a new surge of power reaching me as though something fed her and kept the contact.

I have to go. I paused on a corner, the three demons with me watching my every move. *I'll keep you posted, I promise. But I have to do this.*

The flare of her temper was so unlike her, harkening back to her brief stint as a mean girl after some terrible witches at camp convinced her we were evil. It snapped against me hard enough I felt the source of her power at last and found my heart shriveling in terror at the realization.

Nectar. She was drinking nectar. And not the watered-down stuff from Ostrogotho.

Before I could demand to know what the hell she was thinking, Meira's mind shrieked into mine, slicing across my thoughts so fiercely I had to stop and grip my head in my hands.

THIS IS ALL YOUR FAULT! She poured on the volume and the blame in equal measure, attacking me with words dosed in nectar-fueled magic. *COME BACK NOW!*

I didn't think. Just reacted. And I would always regret it. My magic flashed back over the connection and slammed into her, knocking her back and pinning her where she sat. I had the briefest of glimpses of her sprawled on the deck of a transport with a few demons I didn't know around her before I poured a heap of magic over her and roared in return.

WHAT THE HELL ARE YOU THINKING

DRINKING NECTAR! I lost her a moment as the block in the veil pushed me back but caught her again. *Where is Sassafras? Does he know what you're doing?*

You're making things worse! Meira's mental voice sobbed in bitter frustration.

The pull of Ahbi's magic became an eager jerk. *I have to go,* I sent, chill and furious. *We'll talk about this later.*

Would we. I was going to kick her butt so hard she'd not find it for a week.

And then kill whoever gave her the nectar in the first place.

Meira's power battled against the edge of my mind a moment like a fluttering moth looking for light, only to collapse under the pressure of whatever blocked the veil. Inconvenient as it was, frustrating beyond belief, at least it kept me from screaming things at Meira I didn't mean in a fit of temper.

Small miracles.

Shaking free of my sister's attack, heart now hurting and wanting to go rescue her even though I couldn't if I tried, thanks to the geas, I forced my sister's plight from my mind with the promise I'd find her and fix the mess once Ameline was a dead woman.

My companions ran with me in silence as we leaped onto a departing sidewalk square. I bounced with so much impatience on my toes the platform actually rocked, finally depositing us on the opposite side of the city.

Two streets and a sharp right turn later and I was racing, heart pounding, a roar of fury breaking free of my throat, toward an elevated landing pad where Ameline struggled to force the girl in her grip into the back of a small transport.

She looked up with a snarl, spotted me, hate in her eyes as she pushed the girl toward me. The child stumbled over the stairs, falling into my arms, tripping me up as Ameline leaped into the transport and slammed up the shields. I had just enough time to leap for her, catching the edge of the bubble with my fingertips before she sailed off.

But not happily. *I'm right behind you*, I shot at her.

Damn you, she howled back. *How do you keep finding me?*

Ahbi's laugh slapped her mind. *Watch your back, Ameline.*

Panting, furious and desperately ripping at the edges of the veil for a way to pursue my enemy, I was forced to stand there on the empty launch pad and watch her escape me. Again. For the very, very final and last time.

chapter twenty four

The girl was a trembling, sobbing mess, but when I sat on the stairs and reached for her, she rushed into my arms and hugged me as though she knew me.

It was impossible to get anything out of her for the first minute or so. I carried her down the stairs and back into the street, following Belkni after his short, "This way," which sounded suspiciously like an order but offered a course of action.

I only followed him because I had the girl to worry about. The next time he tried to boss me around, he'd be heading curbside.

A narrow park with a small garden overlooking a waterfall into the lower levels of the city offered a perfect place to regroup. Sassy's sister sat next to me, patting the girl's back as she clung to me for dear life. Ram and Belkni kept a look out as frustration at Ameline's escape made it hard to sit still.

I finally freed the girl's tight grip around my neck and made myself relax, knowing the poor thing was so shaken if I started demanding answers like Ahbi's magic pushed me to do, we wouldn't get anything out of her.

"Y-y-you're Syd," the girl whispered around the hitching of her breath as she fought more sobs. "She h-h-hates you."

No need to ask who "she" was. "The feeling is mutual," I said with a little smile. "Is that why you trusted me?"

She nodded.

Answer number one. So far, so good. "You know me, but I don't know you."

"I'm Tara." Her name came out in a thin little wail. "I'm so scared. I want my Momma."

"I bet." I hugged her again, rocking her a little like I used to do for Meira when she had nightmares. This girl couldn't have been more than eight years old. Okay, demon years? Wasn't sure the translation. But her next words told me she wasn't from around here.

"Can you take me home? Momma and Daddy will be so worried. And Todd's hurt."

She sounded like a human kid. But how was that possible? I examined her carefully as I pushed her back again. Tiny horns in her black hair? Check. Red tinted skin? Check. Black fingernails? Check again. She looked like a demon.

She looked... hang on a second.

"Tara," I said. "Where do you live?"

"1675 Oleander Street," she said as though repeating something she'd been taught to say. "St. Martin, Pennsylvania."

She was like me. Born to a demon parent. It was the only explanation. But how?

"Sweets," I said, "do you look like this at home?"

She shook her head, long hair flying in her face, her ponytail half-undone. "It's scary," she said. "I look awful."

"This is really important, Tara," I said. "Does either your Momma or your Daddy look like this?"

Tara burst into tears. "No," she said. "I'm scared!"

I hugged her to me, tucking her head under my chin. "This is bad," I said. "It has to be how Ameline crossed over."

Sassy's sister touched the girl's hand. "Tara, my name is Avenesequoia. I'm Syd's friend." Stretch. But she hadn't proved otherwise yet. "You said Todd was hurt? Who is Todd?"

Nice of her to catch what I'd let slip.

"My brother," Tara whimpered. "Ameline showed up at our house and had a big fight with Momma then she did something to Todd and he fell over like she hit him only she never touched him." She trembled so violently I had to cling to her to keep her from sliding around on my lap. "I want to go home!"

Sequoia. I shortened her name as I reached for her. *I have to talk to Sass.*

I'll take her. She slid the girl into her own lap, Tara filling the diminutive demon's arms while I paced a few steps away and turned to Ram.

I have to break this hold on the veil, I sent. *I need your help.*

His power reached out to me. *Take what you must.*

Well, that was new. But I wasn't looking this particular gift-demon in the mouth. Instead, I linked my power to his and used him to boost me as I gathered what magic I had and flung it like a stone from a slingshot, my focus on my demon Persian.

Syd! His power caught mine almost immediately, but I felt him slipping even as it did.

Sass. I filled him in as fast as I could, not sure how much reached him as he wavered in and out. I finished with, *Check on the family*, and *We need to talk about Meira*, before shutting down the faint connection and releasing Ram. I hoped the quick shot would alert Sass there was something wrong with my sister, but there was no way of knowing for sure if he understood, or if he even received half of what I sent him. Cursing softly to myself, I turned to find Ram sagged beside me, hands on his knees, face covered in a sheen of sweat. Guilt winning over my normal irritation with him, I patted his back gently.

"Thanks," I said. "Well done."

"Might I ask our next course of action?" Belkni had settled himself against a statue base, ankles crossed, arms too, the mostly silent observer now prodding my nerves.

"I can only guess Ameline somehow stole Tara's brother's power," I said, "and used it to disguise herself. That's how she crossed over." Ahbi wouldn't have been looking for differences in the magic. How many demon/witch combos were there on our plane who knew her personally?

"But why bring Tara?" Avenesequoia still rocked the girl who stared at me with huge eyes, her thumb in her mouth.

"I don't know," I said. "But if Ameline wanted her, I'm more than happy she's with us now." Though it wouldn't be like the evil witch to let the girl go if she hadn't taken what she wanted from her. I crossed to her and crouched, stroking her hair. "Tara, did she tell you why you were here?"

Tara bobbed her head, sliding her thumb free to whisper. "She wanted me to find the power thingie."

"The Node." Ram sighed. "So it's true."

"Thanks for believing me," I shot with sarcasm before turning my attention to Tara again. "Did you help her?"

The girl's face collapsed into more tears. "I didn't know how."

Awesome. "That's great, sweets," I said, patting her hand before rising. No luck for Ameline. But if she didn't have Tara, was there a plan B?

Only one way to find out.

chapter twenty five

Whatever power Ameline used to disguise her path in Bilhaeder, she'd managed to do so again. It didn't take me long to realize she'd laid more false trail, though how she was accomplishing so much diversion I had no idea.

Belkni led us to a rebel house where Tara was laid out on a soft bench and left to sleep while the rest of us were served dinner. I stuffed myself on purpose, keeping my mouth full so I didn't have to talk, poking and prodding at the problem of Ameline and the veil blockage until I gave myself heartburn. I left the table before the others were finished, exiting through the large doorways leading to a wide balcony overlooking the center of the city as it plunged in layers below me.

It wasn't long before I felt Ram's warmth next to me, the heat of his skin pressed to mine as his shoulder brushed me.

"I'm sorry, you know I'm sorry, don't you?" He gazed out over the view, not looking at me, voice aching with regret. "Syd, I never meant for any of this to happen. It wasn't what Ahbi wanted."

Um, what? "What does she have to do with it?" I half-turned to him, a sneaking suspicion growing as he ducked his head before meeting my eyes.

You know what it means, he sent. *I'm not working for the rebellion because I believe in the cause.*

You're an agent for my grandmother. Holy. Just. Holy. *Well, how trustworthy of you, Ram.* Anger spit and hissed in my stomach, adding to the ache from earlier. *So much for your grand ideas and faking offense. I'm sure you're really sorry and that I can believe every word you say from now on.*

I'm telling you so you will trust me. He reached for my hand, tried to pull me toward him, but even my demon, usually so attracted to him, snarled and pushed him away. *I don't want to have any secrets between us anymore.*

Just so you know, I sent, *I have no intention of telling you everything, so you can just go to hell, spy boy.*

Ram's face crumpled, his emotions reaching me easily as he opened his magic and allowed me look inside. *I swear, I've only been working on your grandmother's orders all along. Including when we first met.* He twitched, guilt rolling through him. *Well, that's not exactly true.* A bit of a grin lifted his lips. *I was only supposed to follow you, to observe. Never interact. But that day in the market when I saw you on your first official visit to Demonicon, you looked so beautiful, I had to meet you, even if it meant Ahbi's wrath.*

Nice try, I sent, even as my heart softened a little. Damn it.

I was going to help you when the cousins attacked, he sent, *but I wasn't alone. My partner wouldn't let me.*

Forget it. I turned away from him, tried to focus on the beauty of the city before me, climbing buildings marked with hanging gardens of multi-hues, the whole place its own kind of waterfall of demanity cascading from the sky to deep underground. *It doesn't matter anymore. Grandmother is dead.*

And you're carrying her magic. Ram stepped closer again, hand covering mine on the rail and this time I didn't pull away. *You know I'm speaking the truth.*

Ahbi's power welcomed him, accepted him. Had all along. So I wasn't really all that surprised, now that I thought about it. What was the point of lying to me?

Ram shrugged. *I knew you wouldn't believe me at first. And I figured getting you to Henemordonin was the best way to keep you safe.*

Stupid logical thinking. *Okay, so what if you're working for the other side?* I refused to relent. Besides what did it matter anyway? Why did he care if I hated his stupid guts?

I just wanted you to know I'm loyal to you and your family, he sent. *To you, especially.*

I turned my head, looked up into his eyes, found his

face hovering over mine, closer, closer. My demon had given in to his pleas long ago, begging me to relax and just let him kiss me again, to devour me with his burning demon embrace.

Yeah. Not happening.

A chilling blast of air magic mixed with water power cooled the space between us, making Ram's breath emerge in a puff of white mist.

Thanks for the confession, I sent. *Now if you'll excuse me, I have a job to do.*

I turned on my heel and strode away, leaving him standing there. Felt bad. Hell yeah. Still.

Double "O" Demon could just suck it up.

Tara was still asleep when I checked on her, so I settled in a chair beside her to wait her out.

Ameline tossed, restless, moaning as she twisted and turned on the floor behind the controls of her transport, body flickering from demon to human and back again. One hand fell open, a teardrop-shaped, black rock pressed into her palm. A little boy's screaming denial rose from her, broken off as she sat bolt upright, hand tightening around the stone again. Turned and saw me watching—

I woke with a start, gasping for air, sitting forward in the chair where I'd passed out. Avenesequoia reached over from where she perched next to Tara and squeezed my knee.

"Are you all right?"

I gulped, nodded. "Fine. Just had a bad dream." Ew. And yet, from the furious mix of fear and frustration on Ameline's face, things weren't going as she'd planned.

I'd take that as a win.

Power gathered in a careful thread, I reached for Ameline, trying to follow the dream connection back to her. But she was blocked to me, even more so the veil, the barrier even tighter than before. I pondered the stone from the dream. Could Ameline be using some kind of crystal variant she found here on Demonicon, similar to the one I had back home to tap into my sorcery? If so, maybe she was the one blocking the veil.

But no, that was impossible. No way did she control that kind of magic. Only Ruler had the amount of power needed to keep me from riding the veil or communicating effectively. It had to be Dad I had to thank for my troubles. Why he was keeping such a tight rein I didn't know, could only guess was connected to his battles with the family and the threat of the rebellion.

Damned inconvenient, but I'd have to work around it.

Syd. Sass's voice surged into my head, the 'd' sound fading before strengthening again. *Are you in Nunaresh?*

How did he know that? *I'm not sure if it's safe to tell you,* I sent back, pouring power into the connection. He felt closer, his touch growing in strength a little. *You're on the move?*

Nunaresh was the most logical guess, he sent. *Knowing Ameline would likely want to run under the radar. So I'm coming to you. With Father.*

I met Avenesequoia's eyes. *There's someone with me who would love to see you.*

He didn't comment, urgency burning me even through the weak link. *I contacted the Happerns*, he sent.

The who?

The girl's family, Syd. Keep up. We don't have much time.

Smartass cat. *Okay, go.*

The mother, Taleesharete, is a demon, he sent, confirming what I'd guessed. *Had her effigy smashed, was trapped on our plane. Married a human and had two kids.*

With power, I presume. Had to be or Ameline wouldn't have been interested.

Exactly, he sent. *Human faces, but half demon souls. Like you.*

Wonderful. *The brother?*

Todd was stripped, Syd, Sass sent. *Talee is beside herself, but can't help him. Ameline stole his power so she could disguise herself as a demon.*

Well, he's not giving her an easy time, I sent. Showed him a flash of the dream I'd just had.

That must be what's holding her back, Sass sent, sounding relieved. *But there's more. Much more. And it makes things complicated.*

Okay. I just loved complicated. Story of my life.

Turns out Talee was a Node monitor once upon a time.

Of course she was. Sigh.

Is that how Ameline found out about the Node?

We have no idea, he sent. *She must have dug up the information somewhere. It's not exactly a secret, but also not something we talk about. Some old text maybe.*

I immediately thought of my Sidhe Gatekeeper friend, Liam, with panic gripping my heart. The Sidhe archive he guarded along with the Gate was an enchanted library where every single book ever written was stored through magical means. If Ameline somehow accessed the archive, Liam could be hurt. Or worse. Then we'd be in even more trouble.

I already checked in with Galleytrot, Sass sent. *Liam is fine. So it's unlikely Ameline found her information there.*

Big exhale. *Did Talee tell the kids where the Node is?* Why would Ameline take Tara?

Not exactly, Sass sent, his connection wavering so badly for a moment I feared I'd lose him before returning. *Sorry, Father is trying to boost the signal. At any rate, because Talee was a Node monitor, she carries the residual signature of it in her body.*

Did she transfer that to her kids?

Bingo. Ameline must have stripped Todd thinking he had the most of it being the oldest. But Talee said that wasn't the case. The residue passes better between same genders.

Tara. No wonder Ameline dragged her along. And since Todd was already fighting her, Ameline's power hungry nature wouldn't let her give him up, she just took the girl along.

That's Talee's guess and mine, Sass sent. *How is she?*

Awake, I sent, *but still scared. Would Ameline have discovered the location of the Node and given Tara up for that reason?* Panic pounded spikes of anxiety into my body, driving me to my feet, to action. What action? Not a clue. But I felt the need to do something.

I doubt it, he sent. *If she was there already, Demonicon wouldn't be.*

Right. Phew. Deep breath, Syd.

Any idea why Ameline wants the Node power in the first place? She has Todd's magic. If she can figure out how to dump his spirit, she has what she needs.

Dad has a theory about that, Sass sent. *The stolen magic isn't doing her any good. But the power of the Node... Syd, it's the central core of all Demonicon. Literally, the soul of the planes.*

Okay. That was freaky. *She's trying to steal the soul of the planes? Is that even possible? Why?*

She can't just use magic she's stolen to become maji, he sent. *We think she's trying to become a demon, not just take on the appearance of one.*

Triple-take.

That's insane. Ameline had been stealing magic all along. I knew it wasn't working out that well for her. And it did make total sense she needed a soul to make it happen. Her attempt to steal my vampire from me had proven as much. My big advantage seemed to be the souls I carried came to me willingly, or I was born to them, something Ameline didn't seem capable of understanding.

But, if she succeeded, if she figured out a way to make it work after all, she'd be one step closer to maji.

No argument here, Sass sent. *And while we demons have been known to suffer from short-sightedness when it comes to our own needs*, the sarcasm in his mental voice made me grin, *there are those of us who understand how important it is to keep Ameline from becoming maji. We're all at risk from the sorcerers, and even more from her if she achieves her goals.*

Code for Dad was on my side. Awesome. Relief like a cold shower washed over me. *But we've beaten her.* I found myself grinning at Tara who offered a little smile in return, thumb back in her mouth. *Without the girl, she's screwed. And from the pressure Todd's essence is putting on her, Ameline won't be able to control him much longer. Her lack of a demon soul makes it impossible for her to integrate his magic.*

Don't get cocky. Sass's mental voice cracked like a whip no matter the weakness of the connection. *The boy might not have enough residue in him to lead Ameline right to the Node, but if she gets close enough he does contain what she needs to pinpoint the location.*

Lovely. *So it's a goose chase all over again*, I sent. *I need your father to tell me where it is, Sass.*

He won't, Syd, my demon Persian sent. *I've been on him about it, too. He refuses. But maybe the two of us can force his hand. It's the best I can offer.*

While I appreciated Theridialis's loyalty to the Node monitors, it seemed a bit ridiculous under the circumstances. *Okay*, I sent. *Get your furry butt to Nunaresh. In the meantime, I'm going to trust Ahbi's geas to keep tracking Ameline.*

I'll be in touch.

Hang on. I grasped his power in mine before he could leave me. *Have you seen Meira?*

She's in Ostrogotho with your father. Sass sounded suddenly worried. *Why?*

She's been drinking nectar, Sass, I sent, letting him feel my memory of my sister through our link. *Not the nice kind.* If there was a nice kind. *And from what I felt, she's nowhere near Ostrogotho.*

His cursing faded in and out as his temper rattled his focus. *I'll have someone look into it.*

In the meantime, I sent, *if you can tell Dad to drop the block on the veil, things would be much easier.*

Sass didn't say anything, connection abruptly cut off. I briefly considered reaching for Dad myself, but finally shook my head and dropped the idea. I had my job to do and he had his. I just hoped we both knew what we were doing well enough not to bring the whole house down.

chapter twenty six

Belkni's watchful eyes met mine as I entered the lounge where Tara sat next to Avenesequoia and approached him.

"I need to talk to my grandfather." Not Leader. No nonsense. My intention to make an impression either did the job or not, but Belkni nodded regardless.

"I'll see to it," he said. "About the girl, I presume?"

I wasn't sure if he was referring to Ameline or Tara, but I nodded anyway.

"I have more information he needs," I said. "Some of it might change his mind about his present course of action."

Belkni didn't respond, instead spinning and leaving the room in his long, fluid stride, flowing black hair a rippling rope dangling to his ankles. My demon rumbled happily as she watched him go, while I sighed and rolled my eyes.

What was it with my magical parts? The moment I found myself in danger, they went all one-track mind on me.

I beg your pardon, my vampire sent while Shaylee huffed and my demon chuckled.

Honestly.

I was just sitting down next to Avenesequoia when Belkni returned, but not alone. Henemordonin strode before him, my grandfather's charisma preceding him.

"That didn't take long," I said, irritation rising. He'd been following me, had he?

"We simply chose the same safe house in a time of need," my grandfather said. "I'm pleased to see you again so soon."

"You might not be when you hear what I have to say." I filled him in quickly on the situation, everything Sassafras uncovered and, from the growing concern on Henemordonin's face, I'd finally gotten through to him.

His amber eyes settled on Tara as he spoke in a hushed voice to match my own quiet but urgent tone. "There are things in motion I am unable to stop at this point, Sydlynhamitra." He shook his head, meeting my gaze, looking more like Dad with worry creasing his face. "The rebellion can't be stopped."

"To hell with the rebellion," I said. "I need help with this now." I did, too. Chasing Ameline around on my own was getting me nowhere—or captured, chased, kidnapped at least. And always one step behind her. Having my grandfather's support and firepower behind me could make moving around a little easier.

Then again, now that he'd set off the rebellion, getting around at all could become a problem.

"You can't pull back a little?" I chewed my lower lip as I thought of how Dad would react to an open rebellion. He'd have no choice but to dispense Guards to Nunaresh, independent or not. And that would mean the city would be on lockdown. Something I couldn't have.

Henemordonin looked skeptical, but he sighed and shrugged, slumping just a fraction. How much weight was he carrying on his broad shoulders? For the briefest moment, he looked old, at least for a demon, before he chuckled and nodded.

"For my brave and uncompromising granddaughter," he said, "I'll do what I can."

"You do realize," Avenesequoia spoke up, telling me we hadn't been as circumspect as we'd intended, "this civil war will do its own part to unbalance the Node?" Though delicate in appearance, there was nothing soft in her voice. "The expenditure of power, fighting the old way, draining and turning on demon battle frenzy again... this was our problem in the first place, Leader."

He scowled at her. "I thought you were on the side of right."

"I am." Such fierceness from such a tiny demon. I wouldn't have wanted to face her in a dark alley. "I believe all demons must be equal. But if arriving there means devolving into barbarism to achieve equality, I'm afraid I've sorely misjudged your intentions, Henemordonin."

I caught a quiver of movement out of the corner of my eye, watched as Belkni eased silently forward, face grim but body relaxed. My jaw clenched as I threw up a wall of magic to block him. He turned to meet my eyes, a warning in them, but I ignored it.

"Touch her for expressing her opinion," I said, "and I'll toss you over the balcony and see how many levels you drop before you finally hit something."

Henemordonin waved Belkni off, the bodyguard standing down immediately. "I never wanted this," he grumbled as he began to pace the room. "If Ahbi had only listened to reason. Yet I believe she was listening, near her end." I caught Ram's little smile and short shake of his head. Yeah, I didn't believe that particular lie either. My grandfather spun back on me, hands clasped behind his back, looking every inch a statesman. "I'll do what I can to still the tide of the movement," he said, "but you must know, such an effort could well fail. Now the demons who have long sought freedom have been told to act, it won't be easy to rein them in."

"If anyone can, it's you, Leader." Sequoia met my

eyes. "But we must leave Nunaresh immediately."

"There will be Guards coming." I turned to Belkni. "We need a transport. Something fast."

His eyes flickered to my grandfather before he nodded and left the room. That was irritating. Instead of taking it out on Henemordonin, I instead called on Sassafras.

He touched my mind immediately, much closer this time. *Syd.*

I need to reach Dad, I sent. *Right now.*

Sass didn't argue, simply let me inside his mind. Using his power as a boost and a shield for my own, I reached out for Dad.

It took a moment, but when he responded, his voice came through loud and clear, all the power of Demonicon boosting his range against the block on the veil.

Sassafras? What is it?

Dad. I let him feel me then, absorbed his shock.

Syd. His mind hugged me even as I felt him moving, had the vision of a crowded room full of screaming demons cut off abruptly as he closed a door. *Are you all right? We've been looking everywhere for you.*

Didn't you talk to Sass? More frustration.

I did, he sent. *You think Ameline is trying to steal Node power?*

I'm positive. I filled him in quickly before showing him

who I was with. Dad gasped softly in my head. *I need you to talk to your father*, I sent. *He's set this damned rebellion in motion, but I know if you offer him something he'll back off, Dad.*

Hesitation told me what I needed to know. *Syd*, his mental voice groaned, *I can't. Not yet. I'm barely holding on as it is.* His concern for me cracked, opening his mind to me, showing me how much pressure he was under—his power being pushed and pulled in a million directions as the demons he called family fought for position and his magic. *It's all I can do to keep the peace here. But if Father has started the rebellion...* Dad groaned. *Syd, this is a disaster.*

You think? I scowled at my grandfather who watched with calm. He had to know I was talking to Dad. *Just do what you can to keep things together. I'll deal with Ameline.*

I know you will. He hugged me again. *I wish things were different. I would give anything to have your grandmother back, no matter how I hated her at times, Syd.*

Tell me about it. I squeezed him as hard as I could. *Listen, just on the off-chance it's your doing, can you pull your block on the veil?*

I'm afraid it's not me, he sent, grim and dark. *I've been investigating myself. But I'm under so much attention, it's been difficult to find the source.*

I remembered the stone in Ameline's hand, the one from my dream. *Could it be Ameline?* I sent him an image of the black teardrop. *I think she has some kind of crystal she's using.*

Sorcery doesn't work on Demonicon, Dad sent in a mutter as he focused on what I was showing him. *It has to be something else...* Silence. And then he cursed so long and so loud I wished I could plug my mental ears without risking losing the connection. *I have something to look into,* he finally snarled. *I'll be in touch.*

Dad, I sent. *What?*

Stay safe, he sent. And cut me off.

Hello? Information was helpful. Swearing and dumping me was not.

I let him go, hugging Sass in thanks. *Did you get that?*

I did. He sounded bemused and more than a little pissed off. *I wish I could tell you what that was about.*

No worries, I sent, still staring at Henemordonin. *It's time we pull this thing together. Don't come to Nunaresh.*

But... where then?

I showed him the image of the cave under the waterfall. *Know it?*

Do I, he sent. *I made it.* Smartass cat. *See you there—how soon?*

As soon as possible. I smiled sweetly at my grandfather who narrowed his eyes. *I'll be bringing a special guest.*

Sass let that go when he released me as I crossed the room and continued to smile up at Henemordonin.

"You want to help?" I jerked my thumb over my shoulder toward the exit as Belkni returned. "Come for a ride."

chapter twenty seven

I was sure he'd say no. After all, his little rebellion seemed to be the only thing my grandfather really wanted to worry about. But when he nodded quickly to his bodyguard before meeting my gaze again, Henemordonin surprised me.

"I'm willing to talk to my son," he said. "But the first order of business is the safety of Demonicon."

Wow, that was a quick one-eighty. "Nice to hear you're being sensible," I said. "Which I find incredibly untrustworthy."

My grandfather laughed, a deep, echoing belly laugh that brought tears to his eyes.

"Oh, the Ruler you will make someday," he said.

"Only there will be no Ruler if you have your way," I shot back. "Enough of the fuzzy wuzzy compliments. Time to go."

I didn't bother to wait for his reaction, instead spinning to Ram. "We're heading for your hiding spot," I said. Ram nodded quickly, though his glance over my shoulder at Henemordonin told me my grandfather wasn't so happy being ordered around.

General Sydlynn Didn't Give A Crap.

Move it, soldier.

While Avenesequoia still wrangled Tara with care and grace, we all left the safe house, climbing an outer set of stairs to a large platform on the roof. I gulped back my fear of heights as I slid along the edge of the waiting transport, keeping my eyes from the empty edge of the launch pad though I was certain shields protected us from falling.

Sure they did. I'd heard that before.

A small group of rebels waited next to the hull, but I waved them off before turning on my grandfather. "Not invited," I said.

"And I refuse to go anywhere without an escort." He pointed up, drawing my eye and only then did I notice the three ships floating above us. "For all I know, this is some kind of trap, Sydlynhamitra. While I trust you," sure he did, about as far as he could throw me, which, I supposed, was pretty far considering his size, "your father and the rest of the royal family is another matter entirely."

"Whatever," I said. "If you want to draw attention to us, go for it. But if the Guard ships heading this way notice four transports traveling together they're going to wonder who warrants so much attention."

I hopped the edge of the hull and settled into a chair forming as I began to sit. Loved that about demon magic tech. The curve of the seat fit me perfectly. I'm sure no one missed the fact I was in the front of the transport, next to Ram at the controls. I could almost feel Belkni breathing down the back of my neck. Let him. I was running this particular show.

The shields snapped into place as Ram expertly guided the vessel into the air. He glanced sideways at me, mind reaching for mine.

You're sure this is a good idea?

You have a better one? I shook my head. *I'm tired of following Ameline around. If Sassy's dad can tell me where the Node is before she can track it down, it will be worth the side trip. And maybe this little diplomatic meeting can head off the worst of the rebellion.*

I had a brief flash of worry the geas wouldn't allow me to backtrack after being so close to Ameline, but either the hold of it was weakening or my grandmother's spirit understood I was trying to fulfill the promise she'd forced me into.

Either way, as the transport leveled and shot ahead, three rebel vessels in close formation, the pull remained present, but pain free. Perfect.

Do you believe Henemordonin? Ram sent. *You really think*

he's given in to talks so easily?

Of course not. Now that I knew Ahbi's power wasn't going to tear me apart, I tried to relax for the long trip back to the waterfall outside Ostrogotho territory, knowing I was asking Ram to fly us into the heart of trouble. *But he's here, isn't he?*

Can you shield four transports? Ram looked up at one of them as it hovered over us, a large vessel rivaling the Guard one we'd stolen.

Not a chance, I sent.

Then we'll have to be careful, he sent.

Careful. Okay then.

The moment we left Nunaresh, the afternoon suns rising over us, Ram dipped the transport to the ground and skimmed over it, staying close to the earth. I had to close my eyes we flew so fast, getting a headache from the speed of our pace. A quick look over my shoulder told me the other three vessels had followed suit, so at least we wouldn't stand out too badly. As long as no one looked down.

A bit of a smoke screen, Ram sent. *Can you block us from above?*

Ah. He might have been a creepzilla at times, but he really had a brilliant mind. I couldn't surround four vessels with my shielding—it was just too much pressure with the changes in speeds and imbalance of each transport course correcting. But I could drape us in a powered cloak.

How cool was that?

The world flew by, Ilogabon racing toward us before I knew it. A thin column of smoke rose from the ugly city, making my heart suddenly ache in worry for Culectorion. He might have been a rebel leader, but I liked him and he'd been good to me. Fingers crossed we could get this Ameline thing put to bed in time to stop the rebellion and talk some sense into my grandfather.

Who was I kidding? I was talking about demons, here. Sense? Not much of that going around.

At least I had something to blame for my personal attitude.

It was the last city we saw, passing around a number of small communities in the wilds of Demonicon, over rivers and through a thin mountain pass that almost gave me a heart attack. No more touring of the cities—we were on a straight shot to the waterfall and made impressive time.

Belkni hadn't scrimped on speed for the ship he found us. It couldn't have been two hours later we circled the foaming waters of the falls, pink mist filming over the shielding as we floated down toward the water. Ram guided us carefully through the heavy fall, the same rocking sensation taking us as we passed through and into the cavern.

I stepped out when the bubble collapsed, ignoring the

three rebel ships crowding behind us in the vast cave. We were the first ones to arrive and that made me nervous. Sass should have been here long before us.

They'll be here, Ram sent. *I made good time.*

You did. I sent a little squeeze of thanks his way through our thoughts. *Stay alert.*

No kidding. But he was grinning, despite his comment. I didn't get to shoot anything back, not with the water parting and two small vessels joining us in the cave.

The first one touched down, bubble flickering out as a silver streak of fur leaped to the ground and raced to my side. I bent to catch Sassafras as he propelled himself into my arms, paws over my shoulders, nose against my cheek as he purred so loud my teeth rattled together. I hugged him, let the warmth and comfort of the rumbling sound calm my heart, kissing him gently on the top of the head.

Thanks, Sass, I sent.

He leaned back, touched my cheek with one paw. *You're okay? You really are?*

I almost laughed. *You too, yeah?*

Yes. His amber gaze flickered over my shoulder, ears flattening sideways. *I can't believe you brought him with you.*

I turned to see Henemordonin striding toward us, eyes fixed not on Sass but Theridialis who had hoisted himself over the edge of his transport's hull and huffed his way forward.

He says he wants to talk, I sent.

I'll believe that when his mouth opens, Sass sent. *He's set a trap?*

Probably. I watched the rebel soldiers he'd brought fan out and form a double line beside our transports. *But if he thinks he can take more valuable hostages in this little endeavor, he's got another thing coming.*

Sass's wicked laughter echoed in my head. *Have you been bullying your elders, Sydlynn?*

A little. I gestured to the trembling demon with the doll features who gazed at us in adoration. *But before the whole place goes up, you have a reunion to attend to.*

I set my silver Persian down, watched him cringe, whiskers sagging, tail drooped low as Avenesequoia crouched next to him, stroking his fur.

"Sassafras," she said with clear delight, tears on her cheeks. "I've missed you so."

"Bitty," he said. Stopped. "I guess I'm the itty bitty one now."

She laughed and lifted him into her arms. "I always hated that nick name," she said. "But I don't so much anymore."

Happy reunion or not, I had other things to worry about, leaving my silver Persian with his sister to follow my grandfather. I just reached his side in time to catch half of his demands to Theridialis.

"—Haralthazar to allow us our freedom." The same

old song and dance, sounded like.

Theridialis, much to his credit, didn't flinch or seem flustered. Instead, he bowed his head to my grandfather and offered his hands. "My Ruler is more than willing to discuss the future of Demonicon with you, great and revered Prince Henemordonin. The safety and happiness of all demons is Ruler's first priority."

If Henemordonin was surprised by the response, he didn't show it. Instead, he threw his shoulders back and spread his hands wide. "I am heartened to hear it," he said. "Though I doubt you speak for your Ruler, Theridialis, as much as you have his ear."

"He doesn't," a familiar voice said as Meira appeared over Theridialis's shoulder from the second transport. At least, I thought it was Meira. "But I do." Her eyes met mine a moment.

Fear chilled me to the bone. I had no idea who lived inside my sister, but it wasn't the Meems I knew.

"Meira." I took a step toward her, horrified by the change She glowed with power, and I could smell the taint of nectar on her. It had aged her, matured her features until she looked older than me, filled her out so she rivaled Dad's height. Ahbi's. Broad-shouldered and muscular, magic rippling around her in waves of amber sparks, my sister—if she was still my sister—ignored me as she faced our grandfather down.

"I represent my father," she said. Not our father.

"Ruler's voice is my voice."

Henemordonin glanced at me, a frown pulling his brows together. "As second daughter," he said in his most condescending voice, "your place is behind your sister, child."

Oh. Freaking. Hell. She did *not* like that. Even one little bit. She raised one hand, a cascade of fire falling from her fingertips as she gestured toward the wall of water beside us. The moment she did, a rush of transports filled the space, Guard vehicles blocking our exit.

"By the power of Demonicon," my sister said, "you are all under arrest for conspiring against your Ruler."

chapter twenty eight

What was she thinking? There was no way Meira was acting under Dad's orders. When the tall and attractive demon woman I already suspected of playing both sides joined her, I found out who was pulling her strings.

"Mother?" Sassafras and Avenesequoia both cried out in tandem as Theridialis's face flushed deeper red. Sekaniphestat put her hand on my sister's shoulder, a bit of a reach for her now that Meira had evolved so far, a tight smile on her face as she ignored her children and focused on Henemordonin.

"Did you really think I would ever betray my Ruler?" Her voice purred delight. "He will be most pleased when we deliver his only enemy—his own father—in chains." She moved forward at a sway, hips sending her divided skirt into ripples of motion. "The capture of this ridiculous rebellion's beloved Leader will cement

Haralthazar's leadership. Not to mention my position as his mate."

Oh *hell* no. While I had nothing against being related to Sassafras, there was no way it was happening like this.

"It was you," Ram said, vibrating next to me with so much fury I thought he might attack her physically. "You were the one who sent the Guards after us at every turn. You had Leader's ear and knew we were following."

She smiled, flicked her fingers at him. "Silly boy," she said. "The both of you were so easy to track."

I reached for my sister's mind, found it clouded with nectar, but hyper-focused on Henemordonin. Not me. Maybe I could use that to our advantage. Because as things stood, this whole mess was going downhill in a hurry as a handful of Guard vessels floated in for a landing, the remainder still blocking our way.

I had nothing to do with this, I sent to my grandfather.

I am aware, he sent back, deep mental voice heavy in my head. *It would seem my trusting nature has brought this on myself.* Yeah, right.

He didn't seem too concerned. *I take it you have a plan?* And that I was going to hate it.

I've had one all along. You really think me so foolish as to come unprepared?

Oh boy.

Syd. Sassy's voice reached me, desperate, aching with anxiety. *Meira! She's hooked on outer plane nectar. And something else.*

Figured that out, I sent back, a little harshly. Not his fault, but I was staring at his mother at the time so the blowback to him was inevitable.

Meira's mind and power will be struggling with her evolution, he sent. *This is how she will look, in a few hundred years of development. But she can't handle it yet, Syd.*

She's going to have to, I sent as I reached for Meira and drove my power into her mind.

Wake up, Meems. I flooded her mind with spirit magic, letting my vampire absorb the nectar in her system, a little giddy as the power flowed out of my sister and into me.

She fought me, struggling against the draw on her magic while Henemordonin smiled at Sassy's mom.

"How delightful to finally uncover your true nature, Sekaniphestat," he said at his most genial.

"I've been working to have you destroyed since our beloved Ruler broke your mating," Sekaniphestat said in voice throbbing with emotion. Fake emotion. Went without saying, but... yeah.

"Our beloved Ruler." Henemordonin laughed softly. "You hated Ahbi, and everyone knew it."

Theridialis, caught between the pair, seemed about ready to explode himself, though not at my grandfather, not with his eyes locked on the demon who helped him create his children. If looks could kill, she'd have died about a million times already in varying degrees of agony.

"Mother with an agenda?" Sassafras's sharp voice cut through my focus on Meira as we silently fought over the nectar's hold on her. She glared at me, teeth clenched, fists too, unable to attack or risk losing control while I couldn't break my concentration or risk losing her entirely. I had to trust the others to keep it together for a little while.

Just a little while.

Sekaniphestat's eyes drifted over Sassafras, catching her daughter's gaze before she turned up her nose at her own children and looked away. "My Guards will escort you back to Ostrogotho," she said, "where my future mate will strip you himself before he ends your pathetic lives."

Her Guards? "I think you're getting ahead of yourself, Mother," Sass said, so I didn't have to. Bless him. "You're not Ruler's mate yet."

I know I would have won against my sister. I'm sure of it. I just needed more time. But I realized I'd run out of it as the waterfall exploded in toward us. Ram slammed into me, carrying me to the floor as Belkni did the same to Henemordonin, the two of us landing with echoing grunts under our protectors while rebel ships burst through behind the Guard vessels and opened fire.

Meira shook free of me, power surging again, though weaker this time. But instead of making things better, of clearing her head, I seemed to have turned her to the worse. Shrieking like a banshee over the explosions of fire and demon magic bursting over our heads, she pointed at our grandfather.

"KILL HIM!" Her gaze swept over me, Sassafras, his sister. Ram and Belkni. "KILL THEM ALL!"

Whoa. I rolled aside just as a flaming orb of searing fire crashed into the place I'd vacated, Ram now under me as I fought my way to my feet. My shielding already in place, the edge of the flames instead rippled back toward my sister and Sekaniphestat.

Theridialis scrambled to my side with a speed and agility that shocked me just as a second volley of fire came toward me, absorbed by my shields as I struggled to control my demon's fury. She knew Meira was my sister, but she had a temper.

Yup, yup.

Sydlynn. Theridialis's mind touched mine in a tight beam, wrapping around my thoughts and trapping me so I couldn't escape. *You must pay attention.*

I fought at first, knowing every second counted. But he refused to let me go. I was forced to stand there and take it as my shields were bombarded, Ram quivering next to me, his magic trying to help , but only getting in the way as my earth magic anchored us from sliding along the floor from the pressure of the attack. *This better be good,* I finally snarled at Theridialis.

It is. He opened his own mind then, snapped off a

fragment of his power and shoved it deep into my heart. I felt my entire body pulse once, suddenly as heavy as the entire world and as light as air. My head spun, shields wavering as the shock of the magical recoil from his gift rocked me to the core of my being.

Ram was there to fill in the gap. Lucky, Syd. Lucky.

I couldn't tell you where the Node was, Theridialis sent. *Because I don't know. It's not anywhere. Do you understand?*

No. I pounded my fists against my thighs as the Guards began their approach even as a hail of fire rained down on me from the fight above, a chunk of transport hull bouncing from my shields.

Just let Ahbi's power feel it, Theridialis sent. *She'll understand. And she'll know what to do.*

Whatever that meant. But wait a second. Hang on. What...?

Ahbi's power snapped my control away, snuffling like a bloodhound on a scent, focusing my attention on Sekaniphestat even through the shields. She tasted like—

And my sister. Meira felt like...

Ameline.

The bitch.

But Ahbi's power wasn't done, the pull of our quarry even stronger than before, ignoring all risk, all danger. I turned without will of my own, heading deeper into the cavern while Ram yelled my name and tried to snap me out of it. But I couldn't, wouldn't, not with Ahbi's magic, the soul energy of her geas finally calling me on.

I still heard Meira screaming for our deaths, vaguely registered the battle going on around me, the crashing, burning, violence I was immune to, protected from by the very focus of Ahbi's magic.

And I wasn't alone. I felt others following as I neared the back of the cave. Registered the touch of the stone under my hands as my shields opened to allow me contact with bare rock, slick with moisture, allowed them to enter with me as I reached for the veil and tore it open, slicing through the very rock.

Because I now knew the Node wasn't anywhere on Demonicon. It *was* Demonicon. And only the veil through the earth itself could get me there.

CHAPTER TWENTY NINE

The veil refused to part. It was enough to shake me out of the grip of my grandmother's power. I pounded one fist against the rock, fury replacing control.

The veil was still blocked.

Syd, Sassafras sent, paw on my shoulder as Avenesequoia crowded close. I turned, eyes roving over the fight we'd left behind, the sight of my grandfather leading his soldiers against his own granddaughter and Sekaniphestat, knowing he and his small group of rebels, no matter the backup he brought, didn't stand a chance.

Couldn't be my problem. Not with a group of Guards detaching from the rest to come after us with Meira in the lead. I had to break through the veil.

Had to.

Sass, what do I do? Desperation shifted my focus to the steady presence of my demon Persian.

Open the veil, he sent.

Smartass cat. This was no time for being facetious.

Listen to me, he sent. *Use us. All of us.* I met Ram's eyes, Theridialis's. Avenesequoia's. Little Tara's. She clung to Sassy's sister, tears on her cheeks. *Combined, we have to have enough power to break the hold Ameline has.*

I didn't think. Didn't have time. Not with Meira and her thugs bearing down on us, with Ahbi latching onto Sassy's offer and linking all of us together, spinning me back around, wrenching at the veil with all the strength she could pull from the others. I screamed as my mind exploded, so much passing through it, I gripped my head in both hands, vision rupturing fire as Ahbi forced me to fight the control over the veil.

I was going to die. Any moment now. The pressure, the pain, too much.

Too much.

And it wouldn't relent. Refused. Until Theridialis offered up to Ameline what he offered me, tying himself into the controlling magic, revealing the Node.

The blocking energy collapsed in a rush, the veil tearing wide with a terrible, wet sound, gaping before me, a hole into darkness. I turned and grasped Ram's arm, shoving him through, with no other option but to trust where the veil was leading us. Avenesequoia and Tara were next, Theridialis reaching his hands out to Sassafras, gathering up his son and diving for the gap just as I spun back to join him.

Something impacted my shield as I stepped over, breaking through as my stressed mind gave way, a body impacting mine from behind, carrying us both into the veil.

I'd brought others along with me before, especially at home where I rode the veil all the time. And even here on Demonicon where it was technically illegal to do so. But usually the people with me came willingly. I'd never had to fight inside the veil before.

Unnerving, this silent battle in the dark against the rubber membrane making up the place between worlds. I knew it was Meira, from the touch of her magic, so familiar, so dear to me. Twisted now, darkened, tainted by nectar and something even more sinister, I reached for Meira to calm her only to feel the force of her power reach for me, slamming into me.

With little affect. Her attack died in the quiet of the veil, her magic merely a sting of a spark, reaching me even as I gathered all my power to control her. My energy echoed, hollow and empty too, not even staggering her as she again threw everything she had at me.

Including herself.

The impact of her physical form recoiled through me, though I knew the blow from her larger body would have done serious damage had we been outside the veil. As it was, I found my breath taken away as I tumbled sideways, losing my place in space, falling through the place between planes where I normally flew.

So quiet, there in the darkness, with the press of my sister against me, her power trying over and over to tear me apart while my heart broke for her and I fought for a way to stop her. To recover for both our sakes. I'd been lost in the veil before, was rescued only thanks to the maji Iepa and my dear friend Trill, when I thought I was dead, drained by the vampire Queen Batsheva. But there was no one here on Demonicon I could call out to, not with Ameline in control of the veil.

No way was I going to owe her anything ever again.

Meira's magic tried to wrap around me, smother me. I slid free, not wanting to hurt her but knowing I had to do something before we were both lost. But my magic was as worthless as hers, my vampire hollow, Shaylee with nothing to grasp, my demon roaring her fury into the darkness. My family magic shrank from attacking Meira, though it suffered from her betrayal.

I had nothing. No means to stop this.

And then, I remembered.

Iepa might not have been with me, but I wasn't helpless. Or drained to the point of death. The maji. Veil creators. I had an edge my sister didn't.

I drew on the creation energy, letting it rise to the surface, surround the still-battling Meira in its power. She fought it, though as it sank into her she calmed, stilled.

Creation power flowed inside her as I pulled us to a halt from our spinning fall, cleansing her blood, her body. I cradled her as I focused on Theridialis and the Node, sliding through the veil with purpose once again, holding her against me while she struggled, weaker and weaker, until she finally collapsed just as the veil parted and we stumbled out into fresh air.

Meira fell at my feet, groaning softly, body shrinking to more normal proportions, but face remaining aged, retaining a bit of her advanced evolution despite my efforts. Whites of her eyes showing, Meira lay still on the stone floor as, panting, crouched over her, I looked up to see my friends watching while I fought the need to weep for my poor sister.

"Sequoia," I said, choking on my unshed tears. "Take care of her." I couldn't handle it. Had to act, to do something or I'd fall apart and all of this would be for nothing.

Nothing.

The slim demon nodded immediately, coming to my side as I forced myself to stand, to leave Meira behind. I approached Theridialis, shoving my sister's pain from my heart as a protective measure, only to find Sass's father looked so miserable I wanted to hug him, but didn't have the will.

"Thank you," I said. "You saved our lives, I'm sure of it. And hers." We both knew who I meant.

"You can thank me later, if you still think I'm worth the effort." Sassafras's father crumbled, face compressing in grief. "Oh, Sydlynn, I've betrayed a soul promise and I fear I'll never be forgiven for it."

I squeezed his shoulder, Sassy stroking his father's cheek with one paw where he still sat, cradled in Theridialis's arms. "You did what you had to do," I said.

"Perhaps," the scientist said. "But in doing so, I showed Ameline where to find the Node."

Um. What?

"When I showed the veil where to take us," Theridialis said. "If it was she blocking our travels, it was she who understood the message."

Oh. Right. Damn it.

Damn it.

"And if she's not here yet," I said.

"She will be shortly," Theridialis finished for me.

Just lovely. And yet, this was exactly how things were meant to be, I supposed.

Time to put an end to this and go the hell home.

chapter thirty

I turned from Theridialis to take my first good look around. At nothing. A round chamber, dome just a few feet above my head without doorways, windows, cracks even. Nada. Zippo.

We were trapped.

"Now what?" Sassafras looked around. "What is this place?"

"First level of protection," Theridialis said. "Only Node monitors can find it. If, for some reason, those without true knowledge were to make their way here, they would be truly caught for all eternity."

Before I could panic, I felt the part of Theridialis's magic he'd given me thrumming softly, while Ahbi's magic pulled me gently toward the center of the space. I found myself approaching a small depression in the floor with the portly scientist on one side and the demon girl,

Tara, eyes wide but no longer afraid, on the other. Tara smiled at me, a bright and shining expression before she crouched and poked her finger into the divot in the stone.

The whole room hummed to life, walls pushing back in a rush as a massive shield spread outward from the hole in the floor as though she'd somehow triggered a chain reaction with her single touch. Where once we'd stood in a small arched chamber, we now hovered on the edge of a singing shield stretching upward into the blackness, more black behind us, more to either side.

"Second level," Theridialis said, regret heavy in his voice. "The entry." He sighed, gazing with longing at the shield before us. "I'd forgotten how very overwhelming it is."

He could say that again. I reached out, let my hand slide over the surface of the shield, felt it welcome me, part. A section slid back, revealing light from inside. Only then did I understand—the shield was a mirror, reflecting back at us, while inside the true center of Demonicon awaited.

"And thus the second level," Theridialis said. "If, by some catastrophic means, one not a monitor made it out of their confines, the mirror of the shielding would keep them here, lost and wandering, forevermore."

And while I was sure the Node had been safe for millennia, I knew very well it wasn't safe any longer.

Tara took my hand, tiny fingers wrapping around

mine. "Can we go inside?" She seemed eager at last, her fear gone and, as I felt the pull of Ahbi's magic mingle with the thrum of the Node, I understood why. I felt rather light myself, despite everything. And being born to a Node monitor, Tara must have had more of its residue in her than I had access to.

"We shall," Theridialis said, turning to his daughter. "Bring Meira, and be gentle. I will have the monitors look at her." He offered a sad smile. "Perhaps they can help."

I tried not to get my hopes up, but it was hard. It felt like we'd finally made it, progress, success even. There was no way Ameline beat us here, not with the two protections in her way. She would have to navigate them first and that would take her time.

Fingers crossed.

The only problem? The moment I passed through the shield my feeling of happiness and good will died the moment Ahbi's power jerked against me, pulling me toward a tall metal building in the middle of a bright field. At least, that's the best way I could describe it. The sky, the grass, the dirt, everything, shone white and glowed softly. It should have burned my eyes, like snow-blindness, but instead it made everything sharp and clear.

I practically ran to the large doorway blocked by a blood-red portal, reaching for it before Theridialis could touch it, watching it swing open to the smiling face of a thin demon with a very crooked nose. His smile faded as

I rushed past him, Tara in tow. I spun, turning to the left and the right, looking down identical metal corridors, empty of doorways or windows, lit by flames hovering above, rippling over the ceiling.

"I beg your pardon." The Node monitor's tone turned me around despite Ahbi's insistence. "You're not members of this order." He puffed up a little, though clearly nervous, hands shaking. We'd just rocked his world.

"I am," Theridialis said smoothly. "Or, I was. And this child," he pointed to Tara, "is a descendant." Pause. "And her entourage."

The monitor spluttered, hands flapping in front of him as he backed up a step. "But wait!" He looked like he was about to implode from the shock. "The rest are *common*." His sneer drove my temper to skyrocket. "You must all leave. At *once*."

I didn't have time for this. One of my hands clamped over his upper arm and pulled him toward me as I snarled in his face.

"Listen up," I said. "I need to get to the Node. And you're going to help me."

"But, but, I can't, this is terrible, why are you here?" Terror flooded his eyes. "Please, you must go back. The damage to the balance. Don't you understand?"

"I understand way more than you do," I said, letting him go. "Trust me. Now take me there or get out of the way."

He gaped. Too long. Fine. Trusting Ahbi's power, I spun and marched to the right with the sinking feeling there was more to this place than I was seeing, fairly sure I'd never reach the Node without a guide, but unwilling to stop.

I couldn't. If Ahbi's magic was correct, if the geas was functioning as it should—and I had no reason to believe it wasn't—Ameline was somehow here already and for all I knew, at the Node.

This could all be over very quickly.

Someone puffed their way to my side, Theridialis's hand pulling me back as Tara trotted along happily beside me. "This way." He stopped, touched one of the inner walls. It melted away, leaving a perfectly shaped door behind.

Nice. And good to know. I marched through, into a matching hallway. Almost swore.

"Maze?" I turned to find Theridialis nodding.

"Third protection," he said. "But a Node monitor can make their own path."

Tara was already pressing her hands to the next wall, giggling as it disappeared. "Tickles," she said, fixing me with her sparkling eyes.

At least one of us was having a good time. I turned to see Ram close behind me, face grim. Knowing he had my back actually made me feel better. Sassafras, now on his own four feet, followed close on my right while Avenesequoia floated my sister's unconscious body beside her, taking up the rear.

There was no sign of the Node monitor we'd left behind and that made me nervous. Not because I was afraid of him specifically, but because if he set off some kind of extra protection, we could be in a lot of trouble.

"This way." Theridialis's speed seemed to reinforce my concerns so I followed him, moving as fast as I could, through wall after wall of the maze, barreling our way through until the final one parted and we stepped into a large room.

Full of control panels and Node monitors, one of which I recognized, our crooked-nosed unfriend who tried to block me at the main entry. He hovered, whispering in another scientist's ear. They both turned, all of the monitors spinning with shock on their faces, to stare at us a moment before the demon we'd met at the door pointed with some authority.

"That's them," the nasty little tattletale squeaked.

But the older demon he'd run to caught Theridialis's eyes. And smiled.

Phew. I thought. We could still be in trouble. But smiling worked for me.

Meanwhile, the pull of Ameline was so strong I had to grip my stomach in both hands to keep from groaning.

Give me a bit of slack, please. Ahbi wasn't listening so I turned to my alter egos. *A little help?* I watched the old scientist cross to Theridialis, also smiling, and embrace him as my vampire, Shaylee and my snarling demon smothered the pull of the geas and gave me some relief.

"My old friend." The scientist's smile didn't waver. "Theridialis, you've returned."

"Only to warn you, Bilesterius," my portly demon friend said with great urgency. "The Node is in danger."

"Nonsense." Bilesterius gestured to the control panels where his gathered monitors still stared at us rather than doing their work.

Gawkers pissed me off.

Theridialis gripped his friend's arm in one hand. "Please, I beg you. Is there a new monitor here? One only arrived?"

Bilesterius frowned a little before smiling again. "Why yes," he said. "The daughter of one of our lost ones. Tara, born of Taleesharete." Was it just me or did he have a glazed look on his face? A subtle probing was in order.

Theridialis gestured and Tara approached, smiling shyly. "You've been betrayed, my friend," he said. "This is Tara, daughter of Taleesharete. The demon woman you allowed inside is an imposter."

Bilesterius shuddered as my magic touched him. I could feel her there, her influence, the taint of Ameline, boosted by something I recognized. That I was feeling even now. The Node's power was helping her. But why?

No, wait. Not the Node itself. But something similar. With the same teardrop shape...

"Theridialis," I said, growing fear gnawing at me as much as Ahbi's insistence. "Was there another Node at one time?"

His head jerked around, face paling as though I'd struck him. "Dear flame and fire, no."

Dad had seemed just as upset when he'd learned Ameline managed to block the veil, but didn't say why. No way was I giving Theridialis the chance to keep this vital information to himself.

I needn't have worried. He sagged, hand falling from Bilesterius's arm as he met his friend's eyes.

"The Dead Stone," he said. "Where is it?"

The old scientist flinched. "With Ruler," he said. "As it always has been."

"Dead Stone?" I looked back and forth between them as the pair aged centuries in a few seconds, so pale their veins seemed to jump to the surface of their skin. Bilesterius was sweating, beads standing out on his forehead, hands shaking even more as I prodded the power Ameline had over him.

Node power.

"The first attempt to make a Node," Theridialis said. "It failed."

Sassafras hissed softly. "But the stone of its focus?"

"Still retains great power." Bilesterius nodded slowly,

before shaking his head, color returning to his face. Power surged in his mind, Ameline's control tightening. She must have known I was there, trying to free the scientist from her grip because she pressed down on him so hard he groaned. "Evil one," he hissed at Theridialis, spinning like a striking snake, "why have you betrayed your order?"

The portly demon's grief returned in a heartbeat. "I had no choice," he wailed. "None! The Node is in danger."

"The Node is in perfect balance." Bilesterius clapped his hands. At the sound, a door way opened and four burly looking monitors entered, approaching us with grim expressions. "Take them into custody. They will be executed for defiling the secret of our Node."

Not while I had a say in the matter. I gathered my magic, ready to strike, when Theridialis's desperate voice spoke in my mind.

Sydlynn, no! He met my eyes as he was bound with magic, begging me even as he fell to his knees. *The Node's balance is damaged by foreign magic. This close to it, you could finish Ameline's job for her.*

Now he told me.

I won't let them take me, I snarled back.

Please, don't fight. I watched my friends hesitate, waiting for my first move while the monitors closed slowly in. *We'll find a way out of this. But if you do anything now, this close to the Node, even just with unfamiliar Demon magic, we'll all die.*

Fuming inside, Ahbi's power fighting the rest of me, contained inside a shield to protect the Node, pissed off and out of options, I nodded slowly to my friends and gave myself up.

CHAPTER THIRTY ONE

Another cell, this one big enough for all of us and not all that cell-like, really. I got the impression not to many people just showed up on the doorstep of the Node like we did. As in, none.

I turned to Theridialis, needing to focus on the task at hand and not my unconscious sister lying a few feet away. "I take it they aren't prepared for something like this?"

Theridialis shook his head where he sat on the floor with his back to the wall, sorrow and guilt still weighing him down. "The Node monitor's oath is sacred," he said. Swallowed hard, wiping at his sweating forehead with a shaking hand. "No one has ever broken it."

Shocking for a bunch of power-hungry demons. "Never. Ever."

"I know you find it hard to believe our people have honor," Theridialis said with so much dignity I felt badly for pushing him. "But when it comes to the safety of our planes, Node monitors are absolutely loyal. Only we understand how very fragile our existence is."

I nodded, relented. "So how secure is this place?" I waved my hand over my head so he'd know I meant the room.

"Secure," he said. "But not, I imagine, against a combined assault." His eyes drifted to Tara who sat with her head on Ram's shoulder. Theridialis sighed. "And yes, if we break free, I'm certain we will be able to access the Node. We've passed the main protections. But if we're going to act, we must do so before they decide to remove us back to the surface."

First things first. I paced as Sassafras and Avenesequoia murmured over Meira, unable to look at her. She wasn't my kid sister, not the sweet, kind-hearted, spunky preteen I loved with my whole heart. The monster created with nectar and Ameline's influence through Sekaniphestat didn't even feel like Meems, not really.

But I couldn't run off without knowing if she'd be okay.

Sassafras, tail twitching, finally looked up and met my eyes. "She'll be all right, I think," he said. "Most of the nectar is out of her system now. But I fear things will be worse before they are better."

"Agreed, brother," Avenesequoia said, stroking

245

Meira's face with gentle fingers. My sister looked older than me now, more mature, the body of a woman developed where an eleven-year-old girl's had once been. I choked on the need to sob, to hug my sister and find a way to fix her, keeping myself rigid and under control instead. Thankfully, the need to keep Ahbi's power from driving me insane with agony was enough to distract me from my failure.

Meira was my sister. I should have been able to protect her.

She chose that moment to wake, eyes sliding open, meeting mine. For a second, I thought Sass was right, that Meira was going to be okay after all. The innocence I remembered was still there. Not naiveté. Never that. But Meira always carried a softness about her, a caring tied to a feeling of freshness I adored and leaned on even when I knew it wasn't fair to do so.

The look only lasted long enough to break my heart. Shuttered anger closed in around her edges, cutting me off, bitterness burning behind her gaze as Meira groaned and sat up.

"Where are we?" She refused to look at me then, at anyone, hugging herself as she began to shiver. It was so surreal, to hear my sister's voice come from a grown demon's mouth, to try balancing what I knew to be true and what now was into a whole I could accept.

I turned away so I wouldn't have to look at her, brain

churning, avoiding reality as she moaned behind me while Sassafras answered.

"The Node," he said. "Meira, what happened to you?"

She was silent a long time while I stared at the wall and chewed my bottom lip and ignored the look of pity on Ram's face as he tried to reach for me. I dodged him, pacing again while Meira spoke.

"She said I could help Syd." Meira's voice dropped, lower and deeper than the girl I knew.

"Who 'she'?" Sassafras's soft purring told me he was doing his best to soothe her. But I felt the vibrations in her power, the fight inside her as her body battled the need for more nectar as I cursed Ameline and swore I'd take Meira's suffering out on her hide.

"Sekaniphestat," Meira said, sealing Sassy's mother's fate along with Ameline's. How could I forget the evil demon's plans to steal my father while betraying my grandfather? Okay, so not steal. He wasn't Mom's anymore. But no way was I letting him mate with a snake like her.

And Henemordonin was no angel.

Still.

"You were worried about Syd?" Sassafras's gentle prodding seemed to do the trick.

"No," Meira snapped. Then, "yes. I was really afraid. When we crossed over, you left to be with Dad and I was just there." A soft sob escaped her. "I felt useless, Sass."

"No you weren't," he said as his mind locked on mine. *This is my fault.*

It wasn't. Wasn't.

"I just wanted to save Syd," Meira wailed. "Then Sekaniphestat came to see me, said there was a way I could find Syd and no one else would know. I could save her and fix everything."

Like Ahbi's death? Right. I wished.

"So you agreed," Sassy said. "Meira, what did she do?"

"I was in a lab." She groaned again, so loud I turned at last, with a firm grip on what remained of my heart, refusing to run to her, unable to give her what she needed. Knowing I'd failed her.

"My dear," Theridialis said, "were you underground?"

Meira nodded. She shook violently a moment before stilling, rubbing her arms and legs over and over. Withdrawals. Her skin paled as she swallowed three or four times. "Underground," she repeated.

Theridialis rose from where he'd slumped on the floor to watch, Tara snuggled up beside him. The girl followed as the portly demon then knelt next to Meira and touched her forehead. "She gave you nectar to drink." Not a question as his eyes met mine.

"So awesome." Meira actually perked up, hope crossing her face as she reached for Theridialis. "Do you have some? I'd really love to have some."

"I don't, I'm afraid," he said, ever so gently and Meira fell back with a scowl so dark it scared me. Her power lashed outward at him, bouncing from his shields to hit her, making her squeal in pain.

"Hate you," she hissed. Met my eyes, her adult face full of fury. "This is your fault."

Meira spun, then, her back to all of us, forehead pressed to the stone wall, shaking and muttering and moaning to herself. Theridialis rose, came to my side, taking my hand as his mind connected.

I knew she was running experiments, he sent. *But I never expected... Sydlynn, forgive me my former mate's ambitions. The nectar she gave Meira not only expanded her power, it spurred her evolution and tied her to the addiction so tightly I don't know if she'll ever be entirely free of it.*

And the susceptibility to control? Normal nectar made one loose in the tongue and pliable.

Once Sekaniphestat had Meira addicted, he sent sadly, *she would have done anything for her.*

And Ameline, through association. I sighed, pinching the inside of my arm to keep from crying. I had to stay focused. Yes, this thing with Meira was a mess. Yes, I was a terrible big sister who would burn in hell for not keeping her safe. But I couldn't worry about her right now.

And I couldn't believe I was telling myself so.

We need to get out of here. I slammed the thought into Theridialis, making him grunt. But he nodded in agreement, turning to gesture to Tara. She joined us, looking sadly over her shoulder at my sister before taking Theridialis's hand.

"It's time to go," he said with a smile, restoring Tara's good mood.

"To the Node?" She almost jumped up and down in excitement.

"Exactly." He gestured for me to take her other hand. "Together, pay attention now."

I focused on his mind, watched as he carefully called up the part of him still connected to the Node. Tara mimicked him perfectly while I struggled a little, but finally uncovered the hum again.

They are shielding it, he sent. *So we can't find it. But we know it's there, don't we?* He felt around the edges of the shielding, along the floor, the walls, the ceiling. Stopped in the top corner. A crack. The faintest hairline thread. *You feel it? Excellent.* He sounded like a schoolteacher, but I was drawn in by his patient, calm tone and felt myself relaxing into it. *Now, through here and a little pressure...* the three of us pushed ever so gently, parting the shield, peeling it back and away from the wall. It dissolved at last under the push of our power, leaving the metal wall exposed and ready.

"No more screwing around," I said, releasing Tara.

"I'm going right to the Node."

"And I with you," Theridialis said. "And the little one." He turned to the others. "You must remain behind."

Sassafras was the first to protest, but Ram was the most upset.

"I didn't escort you," like any of this had been an escort, "all the way around Demonicon just to have you put yourself in danger where I can't protect you." And I needed protecting since when? He'd only gotten me in trouble, as far as I remembered. Chose to remember. "I'm coming with you."

So much stubbornness in one demon face. I caught myself smiling, touching his cheek with one hand. "You can't follow." I knew it instinctively, through the power Theridialis gave me.

Sassafras silenced Ram when he tried to hold me back. "Just get this the hell over with," my Persian said. "So we can go home."

"Watch for the guards," Theridialis said. "They won't be able to harm you, and I doubt the threat of death was real." Doubted? "But just in case, be prepared for anything."

Now I really didn't want to leave the others behind. But I didn't have a choice, did I?

Did I?

I drew a breath and met Sassafras's eyes. "Take care

of Meira." Before he could answer, I shoved Ram aside so he couldn't reach me and dove for the wall, the touch of my hand dissolving a door and letting us through.

I spun the moment Tara and Theridialis were free of the hole and touched the wall again. Ram glared at me through the rapidly recovering metal, his eyes not leaving mine until the door finally sealed him inside.

I was going to pay for this. I just knew it.

This way. Theridialis pulled us along, Tara between us, hurrying toward not the wall before us, but another just down the way. Three doorways later and I felt the Node's presence growing, my whole body tingling. Theridialis paused at the final wall, this one's metal pure white, the hallway glowing softly as though the Node itself fed through the barrier.

Last one, he sent. *Be ready. If she's here, we won't have much time to stop her.*

I already knew she was here. Ahbi was positive of it. And the moment I touched the wall to dissolve it, I felt the first tremor in the ground beneath my feet, Shaylee crying out in pain as the earth magic she controlled reacted to the sudden imbalance in the Node keeping the planes together.

Ameline had begun whatever she had planned. Hopefully I was just in time to stop her.

chapter thirty two

When I pressed my hand to the last wall, instead of a doorway, I found myself sliding through the metal directly, as though it absorbed me and spit me out the other side. It was like walking directly into a giant sun, blazing white and pulsing with power. And yet, it only took me a moment for my demon eyes to adjust, the fragment of Theridialis's monitor power attuning my vision to the sight of the Node. I was sure the uninitiated would have been blinded by the spectacle.

And it was a spectacle, so amazing, so beautiful. I stopped in my tracks, mouth gaping open, heart beating in time with the flux of the Node, the pull of its power far stronger than Ahbi's geas could ever be.

Sydlynn, Theridialis sent, gently but with urgency. *I know. I do. But we don't have time.*

Right. Head shake, Hayle. I wrenched my gaze from

the towering, spinning teardrop of light and pulled my demon energy close to me, careful not to let any escape as I scanned the room.

Not what I expected, after all the metal and industrial corridors. We stood in a stone chamber, the walls as polished as the mountain of the Seat, glowing blood red in the piercing light of the Node. The floor felt slick underfoot, the hum of power making the bottoms of my feet tingle. A perfect circle, from what I could tell, the walls curved away around the edge of the Node, suspended in the air over a gaping pit.

She's here, Theridialis sent. *I can feel her.*

Ahbi's magic agreed with him, cutting through the call of the Node. I left him and Tara behind, sliding in my heavy boots as I tried to run around the edge of the floor, forced to slow down when I almost fell. My terror of heights sent warnings and images of us sliding feet first down the pit and to oblivion.

Slow and steady sucked.

I couldn't see anything through the Node, forced to ease around the edge of the chamber, one hand pressed to the polished wall as if that would lend me some kind of support. Pain jabbed me violently in the chest as the Node's color suddenly flickered and turned pink as its song shifted to a discordant hum diving spikes of sound through my head. It wobbled gently before settling again, as the pink faded slowly back to white.

We were running out of time.

I slid further, spotting movement up ahead, stopping to get my bearings. Ameline. It was her, no doubt. But she wasn't alone. Bilesterius was beside her. On his knees. Bleeding while she laughed and gathered some of his blood before licking it from her fingers.

Again the agony, the shudder of power as Bilesterius cried out in time with the Node's shudder.

There was no way to sneak up on her, not now. I'd have to circle around behind her and I just didn't have time. Luck wasn't on my side.

And I couldn't use magic to help me, either.

Please be careful, Theridialis sent. *Any disruption could send the Node into a terminal spin and everything will be lost.*

No wonder they protected it so carefully. And only let certain people monitor it.

The old-fashioned way, it was. Though I knew Ameline would have no reservations using her power against me.

She looked up as I began moving again, catching my gaze with hers. She smiled at me, a bright and shining expression lit by the Node's power as she pressed one hand against Bilesterius's chest.

"Hello, Syd," she said, joy in her voice. "I've been waiting for you." With a laugh that hurt my soul she twisted her hand, power snapping inside the old scientist as she ripped all his magic from him. Theridialis screamed behind me, calling his friend's name, a distant distraction. Ameline swelled with the demon's stolen magic, the Node's bottom-heavy shape wavering as though she'd thrown a stone in a still pond.

I poured my own magic into my shields, protecting the Node from my power while hoping it would be enough. Had to be. Ameline was no match for the energy I carried. Still, as she let Bilesterius fall to his side, eyes gaping and empty, I caught sight of the teardrop of black rock in Ameline's hand and remembered she carried a reinforcement far beyond her own strength.

Ameline glided closer to the Node, the black stone held out toward it, bottom-heavy power swaying again as the ground beneath my feet rumbled and almost sent me sprawling on the smooth floor. I longed to dig in with earth magic, but feared even that little anchoring energy would make things worse.

"You brought her for me," Ameline said, gesturing past me. "Come, Tara. We have work to do."

"Leave her alone," I snarled, skating forward until I was within ten feet of Ameline. She didn't seem worried I was so close. And that made me anxious. "This is between the two of us."

Ameline laughed at me, her arrogance showing. "Oh, Syd," she said, "how very pompous to think this has anything at all to do with you."

"You made it personal," I said, gathering magic

behind my shields, knowing it would do me no good, but not sure what else to do while Theridialis slid into me, one hand on my arm. "That makes it about me."

"Touché." Ameline's laugh died as quickly as it rose. "Now give me the girl and I might let this wretched world survive after all."

Why does she still need her? I sent the message to Theridialis in a blast of desperation.

I don't know, he sent back. *Which means we must protect Tara at all costs.*

Was planning on it anyway. No way was I failing two girls who relied on me.

Ameline's power shot over me, tried to grasp Tara who now clung to my hand. My shielding sent the attacking magic skimming around us, absorbing some, but unable to handle the full pressure of the energy Ameline threw into the attack. I grasped for balance in thin air as the world rocked, Ameline's leftover energy slamming into the side of the Node and shaking the teardrop so violently I thought it would collapse into the pit.

A flicker of fear raced over Ameline's face as she scowled at me, outstretched hand turning to the Node, stone clutched protectively between her fingers. "No matter," she said. "I don't need her after all."

She needs to connect with the Node, Theridialis sent suddenly. *Todd's magic is still fighting her and she didn't dare take Bilesterius's soul on too for fear of losing control of everything.*

She needs Tara to channel the stolen magic so the Node accepts her. If it feels the battle inside her, it could close off to protect itself. An innocent child it won't see as a threat. In fact, it will probably welcome her and give Ameline the power she needs to transform the child's soul into her own, making her a demon.

And if she doesn't use Tara? I slid the girl behind me as I tried another step closer, eyes locked on the stone in Ameline's hand.

If the Node rejects Ameline's power, he sent, *or the boy she's already fighting, we're all dead.*

I just loved his doom and gloom attitude. Made my job so much easier.

Ameline stepped forward, the stone in her hand beginning to glow as she crossed the distance between her and the Node and paused to look over her shoulder at me with an evil smile.

"Are you coming?" With that, she leaped from the edge, over the pit and disappeared into the glowing light of the Node.

No. No way. I couldn't—

Sydlynn, Theridialis sent. *You must. She will destroy us all.* He pressed his power into me. *Take what I have, my monitor power, and use it to shield her. Hurry!*

I shrank back from his offer. I couldn't strip him. What was he thinking?

You must, he sent. *I don't have the power to stop her, but I do have the connection to the Node she's stolen from Bilesterius, but*

I've been gone too long. I'm just not strong enough. He sounded desperate for me to understand. *But with my magic, already tied to the Node, you'll stand a better chance.* The world suddenly shifted to the left, my body bending in half as I struggled to stay upright before it tipped back to normal, the teardrop wobbling. Whatever Ameline was doing inside it was about to turn catastrophic.

I'm sorry. My thoughts came out in a groan as I reached into Theridialis and stripped his power. But instead of fighting me, he gave it up willingly, sagging to the floor with a smile on his face as the core of his magic joined mine peacefully, spirit leaving him to settle quietly inside me.

No stirring monster, at least, just a swell of energy so vast and old it almost felt like Ahbi's.

Mine too. Tara's little hand left mine as she looked up with fierce determination. *It's why Ameline wanted me in the first place. We have to stop her, Syd. And with me and whatever of Momma lives inside me, maybe you can reach Todd.*

I didn't hesitate this time, though my heart ached for her. *I'll give it all back,* I sent. *I swear it.* If that was even possible.

And I drained her, too.

What was I becoming I took what I needed so easily?

Tara and Theridialis now nestled safely inside me, I spun on the Node and drew a breath. I could do this. Could, had to. Move, Syd.

Move.

Frozen in fear, prodded now by so many personalities I felt I might shatter into pieces, my terror kept me still, sweat standing out on my skin, whole body on fire with the absolute rejection of throwing myself over the emptiness beneath the Node—

Until the world tipped forward and I had no choice. With a horrified howl, legs bunching for the leap, I slid to the edge of the pit and pushed off, soaring forward and through the edge of the Node into brilliant white.

chapter thirty three

Floating in perfection, body infused with balanced power, I felt the Node embrace me, its curiosity about me as it studied me carefully and accepted who I was, who Theridialis and Tara were, welcoming me home as though I were a monitor. Until it jerked in pain, its agony my agony, slicing through the magical connection formed from Theridialis's magic and Tara's.

Ameline. I focused on her name and felt myself slide through the light, thrown headfirst at a blackened blob tainting the center of the Node. Threads of sickly gray and red branched out from her, as though she wore a cloak of fiber-thin roots digging their way through the heart of the Node, infecting it. I dove for her, hands outstretched, power gathering, only to feel the Node shudder from me as well, watch more of the taint slide from my fingertips.

Right. No magic against her power.

This was very bad.

Ameline saw me coming, her huge amber eyes fixed on mine, filled with madness as she slung herself forward, the Dead Stone in her right hand. I spun at the last minute, ending up feet out in the thick air/membrane/support of the Node, heavy boots impacting the side of Ameline's jaw before she could correct herself. The Node shook like a quivering drop of water waiting to fall as the blow sent Ameline spinning away, trailing her dirty magic with her. I had no choice but to use magic to stop myself and push me forward again, though I knew doing so did more damage.

No choices.

The song of the Node swelled around me, once sweet and pure, now so discordant it felt like my head would explode from the pressure of the sound, the rush of my blood heating in answer to the harsh tune.

Ameline's burbling laughter drove my anger out to the surface as she spread her arms wide.

You can't stop me, she sent. *All the power of the Node will be mine, will transform me into a demon more powerful than anyone has ever known. And I will watch these planes break apart with great satisfaction, knowing I've hurt you, Sydlynn Hayle.*

Thought it wasn't about me, I sent as I half-swam, half-glided toward her.

A snarl replaced her laugh. *We could share this*, she sent.

I'd heard that argument before. She'd offered help in return for half of the vampire inside me.

You're so original, I sent. *Try another one.*

Ameline shook her head, hair rippling around her as the Dead Stone pulsed in her hand, pulling in power as her taint grew, the Node's song worsening by the second. *Who cares if a self-destructive race falls? They will wipe each other out eventually anyway. And we have a bigger enemy to fight. Sister.*

Shudder. *I can handle the Brotherhood*, I sent. *Without you and your misguided attempt to become maji.*

She shot power at me, absorbed instantly by the Node, but not to good effect. The whole thing shook again and I knew I had only seconds left before this was all over.

The Dead Stone. It was key, had to be. Begging the Node to hold it together just a little longer, I shielded a blast of demon power, Ahbi's magic eager to do the job, and whipped it out toward Ameline's hand.

She tried to dodge, saw it coming, but the thickened gray she'd created seemed to solidify as she did. It slowed her down, almost hardening around her as Ahbi's magic snapped over Ameline's wrist and sent the Dead Stone flying.

I dove for it immediately, the pressure of the flow of energy shifting to deliver the Stone to my hand. It glowed beyond its black heart, a beating thing in my fist as I faced Ameline.

She clutched her wrist, writhing in the confines of the hardened toxins she'd dumped into the Node. Caught by her own greed, Ameline howled her fury at me while I threw a shield around her so she couldn't do any more damage.

Earth magic wrapped around air drove her free of the taint she'd made, green and blue power rolling through the Node. Which bucked like a green-broke horse and began a slow, inevitable tilt to one side. The terror in Ameline's face would have been priceless if my own hadn't matched it. My shield slipped as I released her to reach out to the Node, trying to support it even as Ameline ripped open the veil right there, in the middle of the center of Demonicon's power, and dove for safety, shedding demon magic as she went.

I know about Liam, she sent just as the fissure snapped shut behind her, leaving me with even more fear and a massive mess on my hands.

The Node failed, its slow collapse pressing down on me as the power tilted softly, its song digging holes in my brain, making it hard to concentrate.

I had to save it.

The Dead Stone pulsed in my hand, its heartbeat off tune with the Node's. I reached for it on impulse, feeling the power it absorbed attuned to its new rhythm and let it channel through me, feeding into the stuttering heart of the Node. It seemed nothing happened as I hovered there, heart in my throat, the oozing fall of the Node pulling me sideways.

Sydlynhamitra. Ahbi's voice, soft in my head. *You must find the heart.*

I stopped. Fought to concentrate, feeling at last as the Node beckoned me deeper. I dove down in desperate hope, the Dead Stone held out in front of me, black taint pulled from the white and into the heart of the failing Node, a cloud of gray and red following me down, down into the very core of Demonicon's power.

I bobbed to a stop, the weight of the Node's energy pressing against my body so tightly I feared I'd be crushed to death, but out of choices and time. I called on all of my magic to stabilize the Node, using Theridialis's power, Tara's, and Ahbi's as well as my witch magic and the call of the Sidhe. Only my vampire held back, whispering in my head even as the Node shuddered at the presence of my magic and began to fail again.

Sydlynn, Ahbi whispered. *Foreign magic is illegal on Demonicon for a reason.*

Right. Idiot. I jerked my other powers back, slamming them behind shields, pouring everything I had into the demon magicks inside me.

Better, she sent, the sigh of her voice a mere echo of who she had been.

What do I do now? I reached for her, desperate, hoping she knew because I was barely holding things together.

You must let me go. Ahbi's power pulsed, sliding from me toward the Dead Stone. *A sacrifice must be made. And I'm the one to make it, dear granddaughter.*

Why did I resist all of a sudden? *Will you be all right?* What a stupid, stupid question. She was dead already, wasn't she? And here I was, floating in the heart of the Node keeping Demonicon's planes in balance, talking to her spirit.

Ahbi's power chuckled. *Of all of them*, she sent, *I adored you the most.*

My chest clenched as I released her, Ahbi's power instantly sliding inside the Dead Stone. It blazed with light, the terrible blackness of it shattering apart, flashing it into tiny fragments, exploding, little falling stars, absorbed by the Node.

The heart embraced me as the remains of the Dead Stone and my grandmother's power merged with it, quivered in delight and flooded with brightness. I felt the body of the teardrop solidifying around me, strengthening as the pulse of the core steadied and settled into a slow, heavy beat.

Living. Breathing. Spinning softly and more powerfully than ever, the Node gently thanked me in a murmur of magic. I slid out, deposited on the chamber floor. A further soul joined mine as the energy of the boy, Todd, nestled into my magic, safe and sound.

I looked around to see I was surrounded by people,

monitors with wide eyes, reaching out to touch me, gaping at the Node as though a miracle occurred. And maybe it had. I turned and looked up at it with a smile on my face. I may not have captured Ameline, but I saved the day.

Hell, yeah.

As I spun back to accept the accolades of who had to be eternally grateful demon monitors, something sharp pierced the skin of my neck and, for the second time since I found myself on Demonicon, my vision went fuzzy and slid sideways into darkness while I sighed deeply in understanding at the last second.

Here we go again.

chapter chirty four

When I woke back in the same cell I'd occupied in Ostrogotho, I'm sure they heard me swearing all the way up on the Seat.

We could simply go home now, my vampire sent, her anger a cold fire in my heart while my demon snarled and paced inside me, Shaylee vibrating with rage. They were all in agreement, even my witch magic, longing to be let loose at last.

They were right. I stopped my own travels back and forth the short distance from one side of the cell to the other. I had enough power, unblocked this time around, I knew I could break through the veil and leave on my own. I waffled back and forth between just leaving the whole ungrateful demon race behind and holding on to the need to make sure Dad would be okay. Though, why I cared at this point, after being stuffed into a prison for the second time for a crime I didn't commit, I had no idea.

If nothing else, my worries for Meira held me in my cell, fuming. Pacing. Fuming some more.

My door groaned open, a small, silver ball of fur trotting inside before it slammed shut again. At least they knew better than to restrain my other magicks. That would have signed someone's death warrant. I glared at Sassafras as he hopped delicately over the dirty floor and onto the metal bench, shuddering as he landed on the cold platform.

"This place is hideously familiar," he said. "I hoped to never see the inside of a cell again."

"You and me both," I snapped. "What the hell, Sass?"

He sighed, swiping his pink nose with one paw. "Harry's working on it," he said. "Just be patient."

"I'm done with patient," I said, pulling my in my energy, feeling, as I did, the hum of the Node through the magic I held inside me still. Theridialis. Tara. My grandmother was gone, lost to saving the Node, but those two remained, with Tara's brother Todd for good measure.

I couldn't leave yet. Not without restoring their magic.

Damned conscience.

"I need to find Ameline." Ahbi's geas might have

been broken with the loss of her magic, but my drive to track down the girl and help her find her Maker hadn't lessened. Maybe Ahbi finally rubbed off on me.

"I know," Sass said, purring his soothing way to try to calm me.

Good luck with that.

The door opened again, two Guards on the other side glaring at me. Sassafras let out a soft growl of displeasure.

"Jabuticabron," he said, words as sharp as glass shards.

"Sassafras," one of the Guards answered in a rumbling voice. "It's been a long time, little brother."

Sass snarled and swiped one paw at the hulking Guard while I tried to keep my jaw from unhinging in shock. This was his brother? Avenesequoia's brother? Wow. I was starting to understand Sassy's unhappiness with his parents. Talk about experimenting with the gene pool. "Enough with the platitudes," Sass spat. "I take it Her Highness has been summoned to the Seat?"

Was it just me or did Jabuticabron's face crumple just a little? It was clear from Sassafras's reaction they had been far from friendly with each other. But from the way the big Guard reacted, I wondered if things had changed since Sassy's banishment.

"Princess Sydlynhamitra," Jabuticabron turned to me with a little bow. "Ruler is ready to see you now."

How nice for Ruler. I stormed past Sassy's brother

and his fellow guard, my furry friend at my side, ignoring the pair who trailed behind me, following Sass's lead down the corridor and into a round chamber with a lift in the middle. I shuddered, looking up, imagining the weight of the whole mountain above me as the Guards mounted the platform and it began to rise.

I bent and scooped Sassafras into my arms, holding him close as he began to purr again.

It's going to be fine, he sent. *I promise. Just go with the theatrics.*

My favorite.

It was a long climb to the surface, the air heating from chill damp to warm again as I stepped off the now-immobile elevator and onto a narrow walkway along the edge of the mountain's base. I saw the Parade up ahead, the wide expanse marking the entry to the Seat and felt myself calm a little as the familiar sight of the main platform greeted me, a weeping figure standing on its edge.

Pagomaris hugged me the moment I crossed onto the elevator, sobbing into my hair, squashing Sassafras between us.

"Forgive me, Your Highness," she wept. "I was overcome with grief. I should have known you would never harm Ruler."

I pushed her gently back, forcing a little smile, patting her arm as she dabbed at her tears with the hem of her elaborate cuff.

"I would have doubted, too," I lied, still furious with her, before turning my back and facing the city, forcing myself to confront my fear of falling as the elevator began its majestic rise to the top of the mountain. Sassy's purring helped a bit, my sheer stubbornness refusing to allow me to step back or look away.

It really was beautiful, Ostrogotho, red-tinted skyline fading into deep red and green and gold, the rising moons bathing the edges of the horizon with cool silver. Safe, stable, in balance, did the people of Demonicon know how close they'd come to total destruction? Did I care?

I felt the elevator stop, the soft touch of Pagomaris's hand on my sleeve, but I waited one last moment, taking a long, quiet look over the city, before spinning and marching forward, Sass still in my arms, down the length of the throne room and to my father's Seat.

The family had crowded the edges of the central walk, alternating pushing close to see and pulling back as though I'd turn and attack them. The thought crossed my mind, my temper rising again as I stomped in my heavy boots over the polished stone under the exposed, darkening sky.

Matched my mood. Perfect.

I almost missed a step as my eyes settled on Henemordonin standing at the foot of the thrones, facing me with his hands clasped behind his back, face calm and welcoming. My gaze flickered to Belkni, hovering close, looking none the worse for wear. Dad watched, as stony and still as Ahbi had ever been, though I knew, for him, it was an act. It would be centuries, I figured, before Dad's soul was crushed completely.

Happy thoughts, Syd. Gotta love them.

I came to a stop beside my grandfather, staring up at Dad who nodded slowly to me.

"Sydlynhamitra," he said. "Welcome home, my daughter."

I grit my teeth and held back a rude comment. "Thanks," I managed.

Humor flashed in Dad's eyes. Still alive and kicking in there, as I thought. Instead of addressing me further, he stood from his throne, amber fire cascading from him as he reached out to the family with the power of the Seat.

"Our old ways have almost brought us to ruin," he said in a booming voice, the floor shaking as the mountain answered Dad's words with sympathetic vibrations. "A new day begins for Demonicon, thanks in part to Her Highness, Princess Sydlynhamitra, and the brave souls who fought beside her."

Thought you were a goner, I shot at my grandfather as Dad went on with a flowery speech I was sure would put me to sleep otherwise.

You underestimate me, Henemordonin sent. *I'm hurt.* His mind grinned. *Turned out your father had more loyal Guards in the bunch Sekaniphestat brought with her than not.*

How's the war going? With you in custody and all? I couldn't resist the jab.

Oddly, he sent back with a bit of confusion in his tone, *I was invited.*

Really. What was Dad up to?

It seemed he'd tired of his own speech, because as I refocused on his words, Dad gestured to Henemordonin with one big hand, a fall of sparks spraying outward to bounce from the polished stone floor. "Second Seat has stood empty since the death of Ahbi Sanghamitra," Dad said, grief coloring his voice. "Henemordonin. Father." Dad's eyes locked on my grandfather, his power reaching for the demon before him while Henemordonin actually gasped. "I ask you, for the good of all demonkind, to ascend to the throne and take your place at my side."

I thought, in the next few seconds, half the family would die of collective shock. The outflow of their magic, tied to the gasping and swooning actually made me grin.

Clever, Dad. Oh so clever.

Henemordonin finally gathered himself as I prodded him with my magic.

Seems I'm not the only one underestimating today, I sent.

He didn't respond, instead frowning thoughtfully while I felt his mind churn, physically disguising his rush of thoughts as he tried to understand what was happening and how to turn it to his advantage fully.

"My son," he finally said. "I'm not an aristocrat any longer." Pride rippled through him, through his power where Dad's reached for him. The idiot. "I work for the people."

I would have kicked him in frustration if Dad hadn't had it covered.

"You want change," he said, eyes glowing amber, magic softening as he continued to face his father. "Start from the inside. Help me reform our system peacefully. Bring change all demons can live with."

Don't be an idiot, I shot at my grandfather. *It's the best of both worlds, and you know it.*

Henemordonin's eyes flickered toward me before he laughed softly and took his son's hand. "A novel idea," he said. "Well done, my son. I accept."

"The war is over then?" Dad leaned back, pulling his father up the steps before Henemordonin turned, back to his new—well, old since he'd sat there once before—throne.

"It is." My grandfather sat slowly as Dad did, the two of them landing at the same moment, magic whipping out from the First throne to engulf my grandfather. He didn't flinch, accepting it as it embraced him, absorbed into his body in a flash of light so bright I had to look away.

Dad didn't waste any time or let the family recover from this new development. "Hathenemeira," he boomed. "Come forth, my daughter."

275

I turned with a sharp intake of breath, looking for my sister, guilt and shame rushing back to me. I'd done a good job smothering it, keeping my heart safe, but I now had to face the fact I'd let my sister down.

Ready for the worst, I was shocked to find her looking even more herself than I hoped, though she hadn't returned all the way, more my age in appearance. She focused on Dad, walking to my side, looking straight ahead, refusing to meet my gaze as she raised her chin, now at my height.

"Father," she said, voice soft, but carrying.

"My child," he said, "I need an heir to Second Seat."

She blanched just a bit, only enough for me to see because I was beside her. "I am not worthy," she said. "But I will serve my people with all the honor and power I possess."

What was Dad thinking? Meira was clearly damaged, needing time to recover from her ordeal. My protective big-sister thing kicked in. But before I could say anything, Sassy's voice broke through.

Leave her, he sent. *Syd.*

I missed the extra gasping from the family, only catching the tail end of it as I heard someone whisper, "Sydlynhamitra."

Oh yeah. I thought I was heir? Not that I wanted the damned title. No thanks. Neither did I want it for my vulnerable little sister.

"Sydlynhamitra," Dad said to me as Meira strode up the steps to join him, standing at his side, glittering with power for a moment as his magic linked with hers. "The Seat absolves you of all wrong-doing, knowing you are the savior of your people." Well, finally. "You will be celebrated through the ages, not only as our protector, selflessly putting yourself in danger to protect Demonicon, but for your continued vigilance for all races."

When he put it that way...

"We know you have a different destiny to fulfill," he said. "And we wish you well, promising you all the support Demonicon has to offer you in your struggles."

I bowed my head to Dad, feeling his mind brush mine. *I love you, cupcake*, he sent ever so softly. *Let me watch over your sister.*

Okay then.

"I thank Ruler for his generosity," I said, doing my best to be diplomatic.

Dad nodded to me before looking up, face hardening. "Now," he said in a voice of stone, "bring the traitor forward."

I felt Sassafras tense, hugging him close as I turned, backing off a step as two Guards, one of them her own son, led the stumbling, furious form of Sekaniphestat forward.

Payback's a bitch.

Chapter Thirty Five

No repentance in her, not even a little, as Sassy's mother was dumped on her knees before the thrones. I kept my magic in reserve, just in case, though I knew Dad would never let the attractive scientist act against him.

Still. Better safe than fighting a power-crazed and desperate demon looking to save her own skin.

"Sekaniphestat, Lady of the Fourth Plane," Dad said, "you are accused of aiding a foreign power in entering our plane and using your influence to assist said power to attack the Node which protects our home." Ameline's little helper. How quaint.

So many dark promises to unravel.

One of Dad's hands twitched as though he barely held back the need to choke her to death himself. "You are also accused of attacking the heir to Second Seat and drugging her with illegal substances for your own gain."

No mention of Meira's addiction. She stood solid beside Dad, face a calm mask, so I could only guess what was going on behind the burning in her amber eyes.

If I was Sekaniphestat, I'd have to hope Dad didn't decide to let my sister mete out her own brand of justice.

The scientist sagged just a fraction before her back straightened again as Sassy hissed softly. "I admit my guilt," she said in a voice ringing with passion. "But I only acted to further the power of my Ruler and our world." I knew what was coming before Sekaniphestat tried the oldest trick in the book. "I had no idea the evil Ameline was manipulating me, using power against me to coerce my cooperation." She bowed her head to my father. "I beg you, Ruler, show mercy. I was duped and betrayed by a false demon who promised me your hand." She looked up again, tears artfully trickling down her cheeks. "Who claimed she was your daughter on our first meeting, who lied to me as much as I became a liar. But please, I beg you," she reached out to him, all her false desire on her face, "believe your hand is all I have ever wanted."

Gag me, someone, please, before I said something really, really inappropriate. Or, better yet, gag her and let her choke on it.

"You admit you conspired with Ameline, a witch of the human plane." Dad wasn't softening even a bit.

"I do." Did Sekaniphestat really think she could talk her way out of the inevitable? "By the time she told me who she really was, it was too late to back out. Ahbi was dead and your daughter in prison for the crime." She drew a steadying breath. "The plan was Ameline's from the beginning, to strengthen your position. I brought her across the first time, when she contacted me, using, it turned out, the stolen power of a demon boy." I felt Todd squirm inside me and knew I had to get him and the others out soon. No way was I willing to let three more minds share my head.

Things were crowded enough in there as it was.

"She swore to me I would be a hero of our people once she told me the truth." Okay, well I could buy that one. Ameline was the queen of manipulation. "I accepted because I had no choice, took the risk, only wanting to prove to you, Ruler, Haralthazar," that was gutsy, using his real name, but I guessed she had nothing to lose, "so you would see me for the perfect mate." She crawled forward on her knees, hands clasped under her chin. "Please, my love."

She did *not* just call my dad her love. Did *not*. Before I could rip her apart and scatter her disgustingness all over Ostrogotho, fury feeding my need for her blood, Dad sent a flash of magic over her, crushing her to the floor.

I hoped it hurt. A lot. How dare she? Quivering, thinking of Mom and Dad and how much this sucked, I held in my temper, waiting for Dad to finish her.

"And Her Highness?" Dad's magic jabbed the

groaning demon where she writhed on the floor.

"Also Ameline's idea," Sekaniphestat wailed through her pain. "I needed access to the princess so I could track Sydlynhamitra." She panted a few breaths, Dad easing up on her enough she could speak again. "It was no end of frustration to her how Sydlynhamitra tracked her movements."

"You can blame that on Grandmother," I said, cold and crisp, keeping the boiling rage I felt behind a thick wall of ice so I wouldn't explode. "And her personal power."

Sekaniphestat's eyes flew wide before she moaned softly. "The horrid old creature," she said. "I should have known she wouldn't let death stop her."

The family sighed, recoiling from the fallen demon, whispering among themselves while Dad pulled himself under control. I found myself comparing him to his mother, and knew he had a long way to go to fill her shoes. Which kind of made me happy.

Hopefully, he never would.

"Sekaniphestat," Dad rumbled, magic rolling over the whole room, silencing the watching demons, "you are found guilty by admission and sentenced to be stripped of your power and then killed." He didn't wait, not even a moment, as Sassafras squirmed in my arms, turning his head to press his nose against my shoulder, Dad's power lifting like a great fist and slamming down on the terrified

Sekaniphestat.

I can't watch, Sass whispered as her soul lifted free of her body, jerked loose by Dad's magic to hover over her collapsing form, sightless eyes staring directly at me as she sagged to the floor. *I hated her, Syd. But she was my mother.*

I hugged him, kissed the top of his head as Sassy's brother stepped forward and lifted the empty body of his mother into his arms before bowing to his Ruler and turning, a group of Guards at his back, before marching off.

Sekaniphestat's magic hovered, still free as Dad turned to Meira. "Her magic is yours, my child," he said. "Accept it, as a gift."

Meira shuddered delicately as the demon's power entered her. I watched the monster flare in her eyes, her struggle to regain control of herself barely visible as Dad supported her on one side and Henemordonin copied him on the other. I almost reached for her, but held back.

This was her fight to win.

It only took my sister a few heartbeats to suppress the creature rising to demand more power, the bane of all demons, the reason stripping others was no longer permitted. I remembered the feeling, how I'd fought off my own monster when I'd defeated Cypherion in this very place, wondering then at the gift Theridialis and Tara had given me by voluntarily relinquishing their power.

Meira's shoulders settled as she took control. "My

thanks, Ruler," she said in a voice of steel.

And that was it. I stood there in a sad little daze, heart sore as Dad rose from his throne, Henemordonin copying his son's action, and gestured to the family. The bowed as one before turning and moving off in their tiny, conspiring clumps.

Syd. Dad's mental voice touched mine. *Come. You still have something do.*

I thought of Theridialis as I met my father's eyes. *Has anyone tried this before?* I had no idea what to expect, giving up the power I held inside.

No, he said, blunt and wide open. *But he's my friend. You have to try.*

Like I don't want the same thing. I'm all for it, I shot back. *Let's just hope it works.*

chapter thirty six

I followed Dad and my grandfather, Meira between them, Belkni gliding on the far side, to the back of the throne room and a private elevator I'd not seen before.

Ram stepped from the shadows, bowing to Dad. "Ruler," he said with great respect.

"Rameranselot," Dad said. "Mother told me about you." My father glanced at me before returning his attention to Ram. "I take it your loyalty is not in question?"

"Never, Ruler," Ram said, vibrating with tension.

"I wish that were true of me," Henemordonin said, a little sullen.

Ram didn't flinch, facing down the new Second Seat. "Ahbi saved my life," he said. "Raised and trained me as though I were her own. I owed her everything." His eyes met mine. "As I do her granddaughter."

Don't tell me he'd fallen into some kind of hero worship. Not after I abandoned him back at the Node.

My grandfather grunted softly and sighed. "She was a wretched old creature," he said, "but I loved her still." He set one hand on Ram's shoulder. "And I understand completely."

Dad motioned for Ram to join us. "I take it you've seen to the preparations?"

"I have, Ruler," Ram said, all official. Where was the smirking, wise ass I'd spent so much time with? He turned to catch my eye and winked.

There he was.

Snort.

We dropped into the darkness, Sassafras still in my arms, the lift stopping after only a short trip, a narrow hallway leading to a rough, wooden door. Dad swept it open with magic, the portal echoing hollowly as it impacted stone. Soft yellow light on the other side welcomed us into a lab, much like Theridialis's, but this one windowless and more compact.

I didn't need to be asked or directed, going right to the silent scientist, the round of his portly belly rising and falling with steady breath as he stared, empty, at the ceiling. Sassafras hopped from my arms, settling on his father's chest as I pressed one hand to Theridialis's forehead and drew a breath, calling on his power while Dad hovered over my shoulder.

Would have been easier without the extra pressure, but I guessed I didn't blame him.

It was surprisingly easy, in the end. Theridialis's magic left me as quickly as it had come, oozing out with a snapping sound like a breaking rubber band as it separated from mine and settled back into his body. He blinked a few times before drawing a great gust of air and turning his head to smile up at me.

"Well done, my dear," he said.

I sagged, not from weariness, but in relief as I offered my hand to help him sit up. Sassafras settled in his lap, purring and rubbing his cheek against his father's hand as Theridialis stroked his fur.

"I say," the scientist said with a bright smile, "that's quite the family you have inside your head. However do you wrangle them all?"

I giggled, uncontrolled, feeling my alter egos squirm as they stretched themselves out into the cavity he'd left behind. "You have no idea," I said with a long-suffering sigh even as my demon, vampire and Sidhe princess all protested.

Tara was next, as easy, if not easier, than Theridialis. Her small soul left me in a flash of joy, flooding her body again and, within a moment, she was sitting up, hugging me tightly.

"Thank you," she whispered. "I like your vampire. She's nice."

A delightful child, my vampire sent.

Softy, I sent back before lifting Tara from the slab where she sat. "Ready to go home?"

"Yes, please." Tara rested her head on my shoulder, reminding me so much of Meira when she was little, I found my gaze drifting to my sister who stared at Tara with what looked like fury.

So, she wasn't okay. Not really. I just had to trust Dad to look after her. As much as that sucked.

"Haralthazar," Theridialis said, setting Sassafras down as he faced his ruler, clearly troubled. "We need to protect the Node. This Ameline has proven our methods aren't serving us any longer." Like the rest of the mess in this place.

"I know," Dad said. "I've already appointed you the new head of the monitors. If you'll accept the job. But it will mean even more change, my friend. Like allowing your Ruler to join the order."

"There will be those who fight against it," Theridialis said, resolution crossing his face. "But there are many things about our world that are broken. And it's time to start fixing them."

"The Dead Stone?" Dad's eyes met mine. "What happened to it, Syd?"

Oh yeah. "It's in the Node," I said. "With your mother's power." I hugged Tara, thinking of Ahbi and how she was the real hero in the end. "You don't have to worry about it falling into the wrong hands again." And then, I laughed. "You do realize this means Ahbi's magic is in the Node. And that it's possible her presence will affect it."

Dad grinned. "I have no doubt my mother will somehow find a way to make her presence known," he said. "And it would tickle her completely to be part of the greatest power of Demonicon."

So true.

Dad turned to the right and raised one hand, the veil slicing open easily now that Ameline's control over it was gone with her control of the massive magic of the Dead Stone. "Go home, cupcake," he said, bending to kiss my forehead. "Let us deal with this mess then come for a visit. We have a lot to talk about." *I'm so proud of you*, he added mentally.

Thanks, I sent. *Dad, I'm really worried about Meems.*

I know, he answered as I set Tara down and waited for Sassafras to rub against his father's leg one more time before he joined the smiling girl at the lip of the veil. *I promise I'll take good care of her.*

Before I could cross, Ram closed the distance between us, brushing past his Ruler to grip my face in his hands and kiss me.

And kiss me. Fire burned between us as he opened his magic and let me feel his heart. And the truth of his feelings for me.

Oh dear.

I'm here, he sent. *When you're ready. Sydlynhamitra.*

I caught Dad grinning when Ram stepped back, leaving me breathless, while my grandfather and Theridialis pretended to look elsewhere.

Like I needed more complications. And yet, I smiled at Ram and blew him another kiss on impulse before taking Tara's hand and crossing to the family basement.

Chapter Thirty Seven

I sipped the hot, rich cup of coffee, thick with cream and honey, smiling until my cheeks ached at the happy sight of the family on the sofa across from me. I didn't miss the feeling of Todd squirming around inside me, his spirit and power now back safely where they belonged. I'm not sure what Sassafras told Talee, but the moment she saw me standing on her front step, Tara rushing forward to hug her mother, the stranded demon woman burst into tears, leaving her human husband to lead me to the quiet back bedroom and the still form of their empty son.

It only took moments to restore him, his hazel gaze filling with life before he sat up with a yawn and asked for a snack.

The tall, black-haired Talee, with the wide green eyes and shoulders broader than her husband's, turned to beam at me from the couch as she cuddled her giggling son against her side.

"We can't thank you enough," Taleesharete said, the demon woman reaching out to pull her daughter closer, too, if that was possible while her husband Andrew adjusted his glasses for the millionth time and blinked back tears. Talee's eyes brimmed as well. "I was so sure we'd lost them."

Sassafras stopped lapping at his bowl of cream long enough to purr a few bars. "You have a lovely family," he said. "But you must worry, being so exposed."

"I used to be," Talee said, meeting Andrew's eyes, both with worry on their tired faces. It was pretty clear neither had much sleep since their ordeal started. "But we were complacent, after a while. And when the kids were old enough, we taught them to hide their power." Tara nodded her head while Todd jabbed his sister in her side and giggled. "Since then, we haven't really thought about the dangers." Talee's face crumpled. "I should have been more careful. How did I let this happen?"

I reached for her hand, squeezing it gently. "You had no idea," I said. "And Ameline is a particular kind of horrid." Was she ever. And still evading my search for her. "But I want you to know, you don't have to be alone."

Even her husband perked up at that. "What do you mean?" Talee sniffled, resting her cheek on Tara's hair while her accountant husband hugged Todd. Such ordinary people, with ordinary lives.

And an extraordinary secret.

I glanced at Sassafras who winked slowly. "There's safety in numbers," I said. "And though my people are mostly witches, you're welcome to share the protections of my coven."

It was a big offer and I knew it. Not just for this little family, but for my own. I hadn't brought it up to Gram when I'd returned, or mentioned it to Mom when she grilled me about Meira and Ahbi. I'd been tossing the idea around in my head since I crossed over, though, waiting only long enough for Charlotte to calm down and then turn her back on me in cold fury for leaving her behind.

Like it was my fault. Again. Sigh.

I felt my bodywere hovering even now, silent behind me as I made my offer. I could feel her approval and wondered if the family would be so open. Too late.

We Hayles were nothing if not unconventional.

"Sydlynn," Talee said, crying again, but this time in happiness, "we are honored to accept."

Why did I have the feeling I'd be needing them more than they needed me?

Mom's reaction to our new additions, who arrived a few days later in their packed minivan, was more motherly than Council Leader so I was happy to see her go to Talee and embrace her when the Happerns pulled up.

I was actually a little surprised to see her anywhere but at Meira's bedside, the place she'd ushered my sister after she'd finally crossed the veil from Dad's care and into Mom's waiting arms.

You could have warned me, Mom sent even as she ushered the family into the kitchen as if she still lived here.

It's not your coven anymore. I sent my words softly, not wanting her to take offence even as Gram cackled in our heads.

She waited in the kitchen, glorious in her pale blue dressing gown and bright purple fuzzy socks, white hair waving in wisps around her, hands clasped under her wrinkled chin as her pale blue eyes sparkled at the sight of Talee's hesitant smile.

"Oh goody," Gram said with a wicked chuckle. "Fresh blood."

Mom's answering mental message warmed me up inside. *Silly*, she sent. *I could have made coffee. And cookies.* She smiled at me, touched my cheek as Gram promptly rushed to the refrigerator and pulled out a carton of eggs.

"Breakfast?" She balanced on her toes, eyes roving the newcomers who had no freaking clue what to make of my very odd grandmother. Just the way she liked things, the bratski.

"Gram," I said softly. "It's three in the afternoon."

"Perfect," she winked at Tara and Todd. "Bacon and eggs it is."

I left the smiling family in the care of my grandmother to follow Mom and Sassafras upstairs to Meira's door. The fact my mother was still home and hadn't run off to deal with some Council crisis or another told me volumes.

We paused together at the top of the stairs, staring at Meira's door on the far end of the hall as if none of us wanted to go any further.

"How is she?" I winced at how pathetic my question sounded in my own ears, as if Meira had the flu or something.

Mom's reflexive smile worried me even more than the soft touch her fingertips traced over my hair. "Recovering still," she said. "She's been through so much, Syd." Mom's face crumpled, only for a moment. "I should have been able to protect her."

I'd heard that particular chastisement before, aimed at yours truly by yours truly. "You weren't there," I said softly, hating myself. "I was. And I couldn't," who was I kidding? Didn't, "help."

"Neither did I," Sassafras said, stern and a little snappish. "But blaming ourselves isn't going to help Meira one bit."

I bent and scooped him into my arms, hugging him to

me. "You're right."

"As usual," he said. "Meira will be fine. She's a Hayle. And you Hayle witches are nothing if not survivors."

I squeezed Mom's hand as her other stroked Sassy's fur.

"Let's go see for ourselves, shall we?"

With a heavy heart but the hope of Sassafras's years of knowledge to buoy my spirits, I joined my mother and my demon cat as Mom walked through Meira's door.

chapter thirty eight

One thing was certain, my life was never dull.

Not with a demon family to integrate into my coven while some of the older witches grumbled and fussed and threw around words like, "shocking" and "scandalous". That was, until the Lawrence sisters adopted Taleesharete and the rest of the Happern brood. The dissenters knew better than to cross Estelle and Esther.

Way for the twins to step up.

Mom didn't say a word past welcoming them to the coven, though I knew she'd probably catch some grief once she returned to Harvard and the Council. Still, our unusual family was none of the Council's business and I was happy Mom accepted that.

I knew my grandmother approved by the way she grinned every time someone brought up the demon and her family, after that first breakfast/lunch. Obviously, she approved of the Happerns. And it was always nice of her to have my back.

I took a more active stance in searching for Ameline, but she was doing a great job hiding and I knew I'd only find her when she decided it was time to come out of her stinking hole again. At least I had some warning this time. Her bitter statement, tossed over her shoulder as she left me on Demonicon, was all the warning I needed. Galleytrot, now more paranoid than ever, spent all of his time guarding the entrance to the cavern when he wasn't on Liam's heels, his power so apparent I was afraid even the magically deluded populace of Wilding Springs would start noticing something was up.

I wasn't arguing with the big black dog. Ameline's threats weren't to be taken idly. Though what she meant about knowing about Liam I wasn't sure. She'd met him before, hadn't she? Knew he carried Sidhe power. Not having all the information made me as jumpy as Galleytrot.

Two days after I came home, I received a short email—*Worth a shot*—with the capital "A" under it. While I had no luck finding Ameline, she still had the upper hand in knowing exactly where I was. Though I refused to stop looking, I was resigned to wait her out.

It was a few days more before Meira was anything like herself, though when Mom, Sass and I visited her that afternoon, she smiled and seemed more stable, at least.

She managed to smile and hug us, even meeting my eyes at last, though hers were guarded. When she apologized to me, I let her feel my sorrow and guilt, hoping it would help.

Didn't. Meira quickly retreated and, with little discussion, gathered up her things and vanished with Mom. Who didn't speak a further word about the changes in my sister, but whose face I knew well enough to see the anxiety and fear Mom played close to the vest.

Maybe it was just Meira adjusting to being heir, to accepting more responsibility, but I doubted it. A quick call to Dad told me they'd done what they could for her. The rest of her recovery, her own guilt and frustration tied to the new evolution of her body, was up to her.

What, I had to let my sister deal with it and not try to save her?

That made no sense whatsoever.

One cool thing came from all of this. The moment the veil opened, I felt the Node. It reached for me every time I touched the rubbery membrane between planes, singing softly to me, embracing me and welcoming my presence. I couldn't help but wonder if my grandmother's essence somehow recognized me, or if the living Node simply knew who I was and was grateful in its own way.

I'd take either.

Ahbi's funeral was a massive affair with numerous horrible outfits and endless speeches with a procession from city to city that took three days. I was exhausted by the end, and had to face a furious Charlotte all over again when it was over, but when my grandmother's body was finally delivered to the heart of the mountain in Ostrogotho, I felt my own heart let go of the terrible guilt I'd carried, blaming myself for her death.

She wouldn't have appreciated the sentiment anyway.

I wasn't exactly popular with my Demonicon family anymore, not that I was to begin with. You'd think they'd be grateful I saved their demon asses. But nope. Turned out my efforts to make sure they didn't die in a burning pyre of crumbling planes just drove their jealousy higher. Every demon I passed flinched from me in fear as if I was going to burst into flames and tear out their livers for dinner, or something equally ridiculous. I resisted responding, figuring it made more sense to have them afraid of me and less likely to plot against me than to try to rectify the situation.

Wasn't worth my trouble.

Ram wasn't around those three days and a polite inquiry to Dad won me another knowing grin and a highly irritating excuse about the demon spy being off on an assignment, top secret, hush-hush.

My dad was a total jerk sometimes.

Sassafras and Avenesequoia kept in closer contact now that they'd been reunited and I even caught them talking to their hulking Guard brother, Jabuticabron while

Theridialis hovered and smiled. I knew Sassy didn't consider his father much of one, but it looked to me like their family might be mending fences long knocked down.

Good for them.

It was gut wrenching, at the end of the funeral, to have Dad announce he'd narrowed the field of mate choices to a dozen, the lady demons parading before him like over-dressed peacocks. I glared so hard Dad finally had to ask me to ease up as each of them almost fell to their knees in fear.

Scary Syd was scary. In this case, I was 100% cool with it, thanks.

Now, if only I could scare Ameline enough to make her slip up.

Wishful thinking.

School was just around the corner. Harvard, Liam, Shenka, classes. Maybe even getting to spend more time with Meira now that she was on the mend. Normalcy. Really? How mundane.

I couldn't wait.

Like what you read? Find out more at
pattilarsen.com

Here's a look at the first chapter of
Book Fourteen of the Hayle Coven Novels

UNSEELIE TIES

chapter one

Class bored me. Mostly. How could I possibly take interest in the chain reaction of fire, water, earth and air through tiny little samples on a glass slate when I'd flown with dragons, fought demons and evil witches, battled vampire Queens and almost died doing it? I sighed, chin on my fist as my lab partner, Tippy Meeks, prodded the small clump of dirt to start the show.

"Observe," Mr. Howermall, my Elemental Interactions teacher said in his low, dull voice devoid of anything resembling excitement or enthusiasm. Tippy tossed her thick red hair over one shoulder and crossed her eyes at me. She was the only saving grace in this entire stupid class. "Earth and water are in opposition."

Right. I was supposed to be watching as Tippy's magic nudged the hovering droplet of water over the loose soil, scattering it. Wow. How awesome was that?

Sarcasm, my best friend.

One week into my second year of witches college and I was wishing something really awful would happen just so I'd have an excuse to get out of here.

Tippy winked and fluttered her fingers over the mess she'd made. A little clay man rose from the mix, doing a jig on the glass while giving Mr. Howermall the finger.

Oh my yes. Much, much better.

I pressed both hands over my mouth to stifle my giggling and made a fake angry face at Tippy who let the tiny mud man collapse.

Seriously. This was basic stuff, for babies. Okay, okay, so I hadn't exactly been the best student growing up, but if this was all we got in college, I was so ready to call it a day and head for home.

"Now," Mr. Howermall said, "introduce air to your experiment."

I gestured at Tippy as she raised one hand. My turn. Mr. Howermall wanted air in there, huh? I could handle that. A tiny tornado, danced its way into life, complete with a softly echoing howl. Tippy raised her mud man again and we both nearly collapsed into laughter as the twister lifted him up and spun him like a top. Bits of mud flew out of the tornado to splatter Tippy's shirt. Still giggling, I raised a shield to protect us, too late. She brushed her hand over the tight white t-shirt she wore, the mud falling to the counter under her. "Bite Me" glared back from the pair of ruby lips balanced between her impressive cleavage.

Her voluptuousness always made me wonder if I could do a little enhancement of my own. Not that I was flat or anything, but I felt more than inadequate when I stood next to her.

Then again, I didn't have guys staring at my chest instead of in my eyes. Not that Tippy minded. Thus the t-shirt.

"Excellent." Mr. Howermall didn't even leave his desk to observe us, instead leaning his rounded belly against the back of his chair, face as interested as his voice. "Next, apply fire to the other three and record your findings."

If I didn't get to do something challenging soon, I was going to lose my mind. All of the things that happened to me over the last three years or so left me a little jaded. Okay, more than a little. I leaned back, my good humor fading, and let Tippy introduce fire into the tornado. Mud man shook, expanded and then exploded outward, splattering the inside of the shield with his clayness.

"Ew." Tippy's eyes glittered with wickedness. "Let's do that again."

I laughed softly, keeping my head down, though I was now firmly convinced Mr. Howermall wouldn't have left his desk or noticed we were up to no good even if his ass was on fire. "Thanks, but no thanks."

"You're no fun," she pouted, her wide, full lips pulling down, glowing with lip gloss. And then she smiled and prodded me. "Just kidding," she said. "This is lame."

"Really?" I glared at Mr. Howermall. "I hadn't noticed."

Sashenka Hensley, my roommate and bestie, turned around from two desks up to roll her eyes at me. I would have chosen her for a lab partner in a second, if Mr. Howermall hadn't assigned us. At least I had Tippy. Poor Shenka was stuck with Richard Neuman, a Santos witch. I didn't have anything against him, per se, but he was the clumsiest guy with magic I'd ever met and, after a class stuck beside him last semester dodging flying magic, I felt Shenka's pain, but didn't love her enough to trade places.

She had to learn life sucked sometimes.

Snort.

I watched her carefully handle her clutz partner and my mind went to our conversation from the summer. Shenka's desire to leave her coven led me to talk to her about being my second, something she'd seemed excited about when she mentioned it again at Sunny and Uncle Frank's wedding. But every time I brought it up since starting back to school, she made an excuse or changed the subject.

She changed her mind, was my only guess. And as much as I wanted her to be my second, needed one thanks to Gram's prodding, and knew Shenka was the perfect choice, I understood her reluctance. Her older sister, Tallah, was my friend, one of the only younger witches leading covens that I knew. The last thing I wanted was to make enemies of the Hensley coven by stealing Shenka away. But if she wasn't happy, that had to be detrimental to the family.

Still. I understood. But it made me sad and a little frustrated.

"You've been sighing all class," Tippy whispered as she swept the mess from table with air magic and into the trash. "Either tell me what's up or stop breathing." She winked once, twining a lock of red curls around her finger.

"Things don't always work out the way you want them, I guess." I shrugged. "My grandmother's been pushing me to recruit a second so she can hand off the rest of the family power."

I might as well have told Tippy her favorite rock band stood right behind her. Green eyes lit up and widened, one hand grasping mine, her perfectly manicured and very sharp nails digging into my wrist as she leaned close with a smile growing across her face. I understood my mistake almost immediately.

"Syd," Tippy said, voice quivering with emotion, "I would love. Yes. Love. To audition to be your second. LOVE." She bounced on her stool, still clinging to me.

"I've been wanting to leave my family and make my own mark. And your coven..." she whistled softly before sobering a little. "I know you can't just choose me," she said. "That we'll have to talk about it. But," she grabbed me again, grin as big as ever, "I'd be honored if you'd let me try out."

Like she was applying to be a cheerleader.

Oh boy.

Before I could say anything, a deep, echoing chime rang. Mr. Howermall sighed and actually looked relieved himself. "Dismissed."

I rose and moved to the softly opening door, Tippy chattering away beside me while I inwardly cringed at the thought of having her as my second. I adored her, of course I did. She was one of the few friends I had, chose to have, who didn't judge me or treat me differently. Unlike most of the rest of the student body who were either afraid of me or hated my guts for varying reasons having to do with family attachments.

I let Tippy talk, retreating as I considered the problem. While I wouldn't likely choose her, I knew I did have to make a decision. Any idea of doing what Tallah did and picking my own sister was out of the question. Not only was Meira more demon than I was on the outside, forced to hide her red skin and black horns, not to mention her glowing amber eyes behind a facade of humanity, she and I weren't really on talking terms at the moment.

Ever since her return from Demonicon, Meira was different, darker and more on edge. I hardly blamed her for the change. She'd been purposely hooked on nectar by Sassafras's evil mother, Sekaniphestat, used by Ameline to track and try to stop me from blocking Ameline's way to the Node keeping Demonicon together. And I hadn't been there for Meira, to protect her. To keep her safe.

Guilt, thy name is Syd.

But even if she forgave me, wasn't distant and cold when I managed to track her down, she was now heir to the Second Seat of Demonicon. That position trumped the coven.

My heart hurt thinking about my little sister. Now aged beyond her normal eleven year old appearance thanks to the nectar, Mom decided sending her off to a different school for the year would be a good change for her. Which meant Meira was in Europe, living with Council Leader Applegate. Yes, I could have reached her at any point, even ridden the veil across territories to visit. But she'd made it pretty clear when we'd parted just before I came to Harvard she needed space.

Namely by closing me out completely.

I took the hint and the hit to my guilt and let her go.

Even worse, my ever-present support system, my silver Persian demon boy Sassafras, was on Demonicon for the next few weeks. An invitation to help Dad and my grandfather solidify their new rule wasn't something he could turn down. As much as I knew it was a huge honor and Sass was excited to go, I missed him every single day.

He deserved a life. Of course he did. I just wished he could live it around me at the moment.

I caught Shenka's eye as we cleared the exit to Coven Hall and passed through to the library, on our way to lunch. She smiled, slowed to wait for me, even as my gaze drifted past her to a girl with long, black hair.

Ameline. No, of course not. The girl turned to smile at her companion, showing me her profile. Not my nemesis. And yet, the reminder was a jab to my guts and, I knew, the source of my discontent with going to college.

What did school matter when I should be out there hunting Ameline Benoit down?

And killing her.

About the Author

Everything you need to know about me is in this one statement: I've wanted to be a writer since I was a little girl, and now I'm doing it. How cool is that, being able to follow your dream and make it reality? I've tried everything from university to college, graduating the second with a journalism diploma (I sucked at telling real stories), am part of an all-girl improv troupe (if you've never tried it, I highly recommend making things up as you go along as often as possible). I've even been in a Celtic girl band (some of our stuff is on YouTube!) and was an independent film maker. My life has been one creative thing after another—all leading me here, to writing books for a living.

Now with multiple series in happy publication, I live on beautiful and magical Prince Edward Island (I know you've heard of Anne of Green Gables) with my very patient husband and multitude of pets.

I love-love-love hearing from you! You can reach me (and I promise I'll message back) at patti@pattilarsen.com. And if you're eager for your next dose of Patti Larsen books (usually about one release a month) come join my mailing list! All the best up and coming, giveaways, contests and, of course, my observations on the world (aren't you just dying to know what I think about everything?) all in one place: http://smarturl.it/PattiLarsenEmail.

Last—but not least!—I hope you enjoyed what you read! Your happiness is my happiness. And I'd love to hear just what you thought. A review where you found this book would mean the world to me—reviews feed writers more than you will ever know. So, loved it (or not so much), **your honest review would make my day**. Thank you!

www.ingramcontent.com/pod-product-compliance
Lightning Source LLC
Chambersburg PA
CBHW060524180626
46817CB00002B/481